NEPHILIM
THE
REMEMBERING

Written by
Kirk Allen Kreitzer

iUniverse, Inc.
Bloomington

Nephilim The Remembering

iUniverse books may be ordered through booksellers or by contacting:

iUniverse
1663 Liberty Drive
Bloomington, IN 47403
www.iuniverse.com
1-800-Authors (1-800-288-4677)

Because of the dynamic nature of the Internet, any web addresses or links contained in this book may have changed since publication and may no longer be valid. The views expressed in this work are solely those of the author and do not necessarily reflect the views of the publisher, and the publisher hereby disclaims any responsibility for them.

Any people depicted in stock imagery provided by Thinkstock are models, and such images are being used for illustrative purposes only.

Certain stock imagery © Thinkstock.

ISBN: 978-1-4620-3391-1 (sc)
ISBN: 978-1-4620-3392-8 (e)
ISBN: 978-1-4620-3393-5 (dj)

Printed in the United States of America

iUniverse rev. date: 11/1/2011

A letter from the author:

Nephilim – The Remembering is my very first attempt at any sustained writing (beyond the uber complex: *Honey- gone to the store. Back in 15 min*). I see it as a Stephen King meets Dan Brown.

I never would have believed how freeing writing is. For once letting my unproductive but personally entertaining daydreams come to life for others to share and enjoy was... well productive and personally entertaining. A couple hours at a time sitting in the library with only me and my new best friends (Curtis, Eavery and the group), and a pen and paper — yep, I did it old school.

It's wild, but there were even times while I was writing I scared myself or I felt so bad (John's mother) that I would go and steal a kiss and hug from my wife, Lisa. I know the countless hours I took for myself in this new endeavour was difficult on my family — after all, I had to write after work and on weekends (on top of the 10 weeks the air force sent me out of the province).

So I offer a toast, to what I know will be a lucrative and fantastic career as an author, to my wife, Lisa — thanks for the reads, the re-reads, the editing and the overall just-putting-up-with-me. To my parents, Don and Rose and my sisters Cheryl, Dianne, and Lori for sharing in my excitement and to my Texan Uncle John for buying a copy before I was even finished writing it. And a small cheer to my little pumpkin Alexsys: sorry for hogging the computer and not giving you the full attention a four/five year old needs.

Oh, what the hell! And here's a toast to you, for giving my story *Nephilim: The Remembering* a chance. You hear this all the time, but I mean it — if you enjoy reading it half as much as I enjoyed having my own personal time to write it, I think you're going to love it.

See ya at the end....

CHAPTER ONE

El Omari, Lower Egypt. 3700 BC

The night air was cooler than the last several, but it was more refreshing than unpleasant — an excellent night for offerings and prayers. Memlis bent over and filled a pouch made from dried fish skins with sand and ashes from a consecrated fire that was still smoldering. As the bright moon began to rise above the horizon, the holy man, wearing his ceremonial wrap and strung beads dipped his right hand into the pouch. Facing north, he stretched out his arm and prayed for a healthy harvest to the Sacred Breath, allowing the purified earth to run through his fingers and blessing all the land to the north. For three years, his tribe has faced many hardships from the flooding of their noble river. He continued the blessings facing east, south and west. Nunchintet, the tribe's high priest and Memlis's father, knelt down at an already ancient altar made of sandstone. Undoing a shoulder bag tied across his chest, he poured milk into a bowl made from woven reeds and sealed with beeswax. He held the bowl of milk, symbolizing the full, harvest moon in both hands, and looked up to the bright celestial orb.

"Offerings to you, Oh Great One," he said as he poured

1

the milk onto the altar. "I ask for wisdom and knowledge of the earth, and of the heavens, for this life and the next."

In the puddle of milk, Nunchintet took a reed that had been frayed on the one end. He began to sketch a picture of mountains and palm trees framed within a square. Then, a second frame with a moon surrounded by dots and finally a third with one stick figure walking towards an open door, as another figure walked away from the door. Nunchintet bowed his head and raised both his hands up to the moon.

"Goddess, I am Nunchintet thy servant, command thee, and share thy great wisdom." Nunchintet's head began to spin and he had to reach out to the sandstone table to steady himself.

"I must have eaten something that has set my head a spin," Memlis said aloud behind him, expressing their shared physical symptoms and mimicking Nunchintet's own thoughts. Then both of their hearts began to race. A curse that has been spreading throughout the other tribes may have finally reached theirs.

No, Nunchintet thought, centering himself. *This has come about too quickly.*

The high priest felt as if he was in mortal danger, and his instincts were telling him to leave the altar. Just then the moon began to glow brighter. It continued until it had the brilliance of the sun at midday but without any of its searing heat. Memlis, dropping his sacred pouch of ash and earth at his feet, shielded his eyes with his hands, and he quickly knelt down beside his priestly father at the altar. Together they chanted for forgiveness and mercy. Suddenly, a crack of lightning lit up the area around the two men, and a thunderous blast echoed off the limestone mountain range hundreds of kilometers away. Both men, too afraid to open their eyes, continued to pray with their palms up in a surrendering pose.

Then a voice took on a sound as if all the stars in the

universe sang in harmony, like an orchestra playing the same note and covering all octaves. It flowed in and out of the ground. It passed through the altar, and penetrated the two men. Jackals and wild animals off in the distance joined in the chorus. The two priests were overwhelmed with emotions: love, hate, joy, sorrow. They swelled with memories from their childhood, both the wonderful and the tragic. Then it stopped abruptly, leaving them cold and alone, as if they were naked standing within a room of strangers. When they opened their eyes, a giant of a man stood before them. His skin looked metallic, like a mixture of liquid mercury and gold flakes. The giant easily stood taller than the two priests combined. He had the head of an Ibis bird, with a long narrow beak. From his waste to his knees, he was covered in a silk wrap that had golden symbols embroidered throughout it. In his left hand he held a scroll.

The priest's senses were confused. The Being glistened like the sun striking the water on a moving brook, or a sudden release of stray sparks from dried twigs set aflame. The air held the scent similar to the air after a violent lightning storm.

The marvelous creature exuded power. It radiated strength; both gentle and terrifying, filling the men with a sense of invulnerability that can be imaged when having thousands of soldiers standing at your side.

"I am Thoth," the giant said. "Lord of the Heavens. Beautiful of Night. I am God of Learning and Wisdom."

Nunchintet raised his gaze to Thoth. "Lord Thoth, what dost thou command thy servant?"

Thoth looked down at both priests. Contact with the mortals was forbidden, but he and the others had been watching them stumble blindly for a millennia, and he pitied them. Ever since the First One had lost his favour with the Creator, his children have suffered.

"Your deeds and prayers have been witnessed by the God of Gods," he lied. "And you have been honoured as His chosen people. I will grant you wisdom and knowledge of the sacred language spoken in the heavens, so that your mind can think it, your tongue will speak it, and your hands will scribe it to papyrus and chisel it in stone. You will pass this wisdom to your brothers and sons. But guard it, for as long as you hold this knowledge, your people will flourish and your nation will be the greatest nation among nations."

CHAPTER TWO

And Moses by the commandment of the LORD sent them from the wilderness of Paran: all those men were heads of the children of Israel... And Moses sent them to spy out the land of Canaan, and said unto them, Get you up this way southward, and go up into the mountain: And see the land, what it is, and the people that dwelleth therein, whether they be strong or weak, few or many; And what the land is that they dwell in, whether it be good or bad; and what cities they be that they dwell in, whether in tents, or in strong holds; And they ascended by the south, and came unto Hebron; where Ahiman, Sheshai, and Talmai, the children of Anak, were there.

Numbers 13

Kiriath Arba (Hebron), 1325 BC.
Palace of Arba

Both doors of the Great Hall violently swung open. A large man wearing a bronze helmet with wings carved on the sides, holding a giant shield in his left arm and a shaft with a sharpened bronze tip in his right, quickly walked past the sixteen marble pillars (eight per side). Between each pillar were lit drums of oil hanging from a colossal ceiling casting glowing warmth throughout the cavernous hall.

At the far end of the hall were two giant marble statues. Chiseled within the base of each statue, in a strange symbolic language alien to most visitors and guests, were ARBA and ANAK. Both figures had solid gold wings sprouting out their back. In between the two figures was a large throne made of polished cherry wood. Adorning the feet of the throne were paws of a lion made of gold. The sides of the throne bore a gold disk with wings etched into it, similar to the design on the shield.

The man with the shield excitedly yelled down the hall, "Brother, we will soon be under attack."

"Ahiman," said the man sitting on the throne. "Is this how thou greets thy brother? No blessings? No peace granted?"

With a large smile on his face he looked to his servant far off to his right. "Rabdebar, bring my brother wine and meat. Begin kneading the flour, tonight the Gods have favoured us. We feast!"

"No, Sheshai!" cries Ahiman, angry his brother is not heeding his words. "Tonight we prepare for war." Sheshai, looking perplexed, stands to greet his brother.

"Brother, what curses have caused thou to be so excited. Have the marketers haggled thou unfairly again this harvest?" Sheshai asks, slapping his brother in the arm.

"Let us eat and drink. I haven't seen or heard word in two full moons, and nothing of thy family. How is Rachima, my brother's wife? And my brother's son, Bedezee, he must be almost..."

"Sheshai!" his brother cuts him off. "Talmai has been killed!"

"What?" A look of concern spread across the elder brother's face. Talmai was the youngest and more adventurous of the three Nephilim princes. He was also the largest of the royal giants; three times the size of a full grown man.

"What is this news of our brother thou speaks?"

With the weight of his message, the exhaustion of three days of straight travel and the loss of his brother, Ahiman's excited stance drained from him. He shifted his eyes from the floor back to his older brother.

"He went ahead of us to meet Anak and Arba while he was lying with his wife."

Now fully into focus, Sheshai asks, "Who did this? How has thou come into this knowledge?"

"Bartal, our brother's eldest, fled from his palace and came to me as all of Talmai's land was set aflame. He barely escaped, ran on foot the full way — two days' length by chariot."

Just then the servant Rabdebar approached the throne with two men carrying a large table with a flask of wine and a roasted pig. He looked like a child next to the two serving men that stood almost three meters tall. The two giant servants were still a full head shorter than the royal brothers.

"Who did this?" Sheshai asks his brother. "And why?"

Looking towards the servants he softened his tone. "Bring water, we will need a clear head tonight."

Sheshai grabbed the shield and staff from his brother and leaned them against the throne. "Eat brother, we will need our strength."

Eager to eat, Ahiman grabbed the thigh of the beast and pulled it easily away.

"The Hebrew slaves from Egypt did this," Ahiman said as he took a bite of the leg, the tender meat filling his mouth.

"Those men whom were greeted and fed at the brook of Eshcol some thirty harvests past?" Sheshai asked trying to thinking back.

"The same," Ahiman muffled between stuffed cheeks. He dipped his chalice into a large caldron of water the servants had just brought out. Taking a drink to clear his mouth and coughing at his own gluttony, "Joshua, son of Nun, and Caleb, son of Jophunneh, have been plaguing the land. They have

7

conquered the east bank of the Sea of The Arabah, from the River of Arnon to the land of Bashan."

Sheshai looked down at his brother's shield and staff. "Bashan?"

Ahiman wiped his mouth on a silk cloth provided at the table. "They have destroyed the cities of Aroer, Gilead and Bashan. They killed the Great King Og and slaughtered all of his people, even their wives and children. They have taken their flocks of sheep and any gold, whether it be fastened down or less."

Sheshai reached down and grabbed Ahiman's staff in his mighty hand, feeling its weight, the density of the wood. He stared at his distorted reflection on the polished bronze tip; a tip that had never seen battle, a tip that had never drawn blood. A feeling of rage and a sense of desperation began to well up inside the giant.

"Why? We have flourished here for thousands of harvests. We have marketed and celebrated life with man. We have honoured their women and given them great sons. Why would these slaves take land that is rightfully ours?" Looking at Ahiman he clenched his jaws and squeezed his mighty hand around the stem of the staff. "How could they? How was it even possible?"

Then he thought, *Our cities have great walls that tower over them. How can the simple tribes of man defeat a Nephilim city? Surely, the great tribes of Zamzummins have not been defeated, a tribe far greater than our own.*

Ahiman reached into a sack that was strapped across his chest and fitted under the arm and pulled out a small rolled up papyrus map, and as if hearing his brother's thoughts continued, "They have all been taken. Bartal, killed a man while escaping and the man was carrying this scroll. It describes in detail the lands of Edom, Moab, Ammon, Bashan and Canaan."

Sheshai, still holding the staff, slammed the blunt end against the marble floor with rage. "So that Joshua was a spy and his kind words were false."

"That is not all, brother," Ahiman said as he walked away from the table. Even though he had not eaten in several days, the gravity of the situation killed his appetite. "Bartal overheard some of Joshua's men speaking to each other. They say they cannot lose because Joshua's leader speaks directly to Yahweh."

"What?" Sheshai shouted. "Yahweh speaks directly to no man. Even the blessed man Noah was guided by the *Malakh Adonai*, one of only seven Angels of Presence that have actually seen the face of Yahweh."

Ahiman reached over and grabbed his brother's arm. "It matters little which Elohim has tricked their leader... Moses," he said searching for the name. "His people are encouraged and they fight like wild dogs pulling meat from a fresh kill. When men believe themselves to be truly blessed, they will take whatever prize they feel they are entitled."

Sheshai turned and looked up at the statues of his father and grandfather. Still holding the spear he knelt down. "Anak, Arba, hear my words. The glory days of battle have not honoured thy sons as they have honoured thou. We have had no need for it. Those glories have died with thou. But that time has come once again. Grant me thy hand and heart that I may lead the children of Arba against this enemy that dishonours thy name."

As Sheshai finished his prayer, the ceiling high above the throne began to shimmer like looking through the heat trails escaping off a hot surface. The distortion descended and before the brothers eyes a form of golden static started to take shape. The hall was filled with the sound of raw electricity. Small arcs reached the gold tips of the throne and fingered out a meter in all directions on the marble floor. A large intense flash engulfed the princes. When the brothers looked up they met the eyes of a large majestic figure standing at the base of the throne. The being emitted an energy that was felt more than seen. It was ancient and peaceful but a sense of dominance radiated from it. The divine spark that is part of the soul understood this creature to be loving *and* deadly.

Immediately Ahiman knelt down beside his brother and the two bowed their heads.

"Sheshai, Ahiman. Stand! I am Uriel."

The two royal brothers stood. The Archangel was a golden, almost translucent giant. He stood five meters tall and the surface of his body seemed to flow and wave like the bottom of a pool of water. "Your prayers have not fallen on deaf ears proud Nephilim."

Sheshai's sense of urgency was beginning to overtake his sense of awe and respect. "Please, cousin, grant us the sword to smite those that dost dishonour thy children."

The archangel looked down at Sheshai. "The time of the Nephilim have come and gone Sheshai. Your dominant reign has lasted 2000 years, but will not carry on until morning."

Just then Rabdebar the servant approached the throne in a hysteric fury. Seeing only the two brothers and not the angel he ran to Sheshai.

"Your Highness!" the servant barely got out. "The city is aflame. Men are coming over the city's walls, killing everyone."

Sheshai put his hand on the servant's shoulder, covering it like a father would his adolescent son. Rabdebar, born into slavery like his parents before him, was ready to fight with honour at his master's side.

"Go Rabdebar, if thou can. Take thy family and leave Kiriath Arba. Thou art free." Rabdebar touched his former master's hand and then left quickly out the servant's door for the last time.

"He was blind to thou?" Ahiman asked Uriel.

Uriel nodded. "Yes, only those whose eyes have been

opened can see us, only those who hold the knowledge. You, Nephilim, have been conceived with divine seed within a human woman. You will always hold the sacred knowledge. Now, you must send away your children and give them as much of the library as they can carry, so that your knowledge and seed will live on."

A large pounding reverberated from the massive doors at the front of the Great Hall. Axes and fists were slamming against the mighty oak frame. Sheshai turned towards Ahiman.

"Brother, thou must leave the Great Hall from the servant's entrance. Save my family."

Ahiman stared into his brother's grief-stricken face, knowing what he is being asked to do.

"Sheshai, that door will hold but a minute. Thou go and save *thy* family. I know mine is already lost and I long to meet them."

Ahiman bent down, grabbed his shield and reached for the spear already in Sheshai's hand. Sheshai shifted the spear so he couldn't grab it.

"NO, Ahiman!" Sheshai hollered a little louder than he meant to, but the situation of his family and the fate of what was about to occur had caused desperation.

Holding his arms wide, he said, "This is my land. I will defend it. Thou must protect my family, our family, our knowledge, and our scrolls. Teach my son the prayers our father taught us, the ones I failed to teach him. Tell him that I thought I had more time."

With another smash a large crack split up the centre of the right door.

"Go brother, please!" Sheshai pleaded with desperation in his voice. Ahiman truly wanted to be with his brother but he fully understood that someone must save their history. He reached over and gave his brother the winged shield. Without another word he turned and exited out the servant's way. As

Sheshai watched his brother leave he felt alone. And, although he had great size, much larger than that of the humans, he felt small.

His grandfather, Anak, had a rule he lived by: *When thou lives-live grand and stand tall. And when thou fall- fall alone.*

Sheshai never understood Anak's mysterious proverbs, until today. He had never put much thought into death — not really, not like this. He had thought death would come while he slept, comfortable in his royal night chamber, holding his beloved wife. He had fantasized his kingdom would weep and then hold a great festival and parade. Merriment and love-making would carry on until the next morning when they would all toast his name: *SHESHAI.*

That is how Nephilim princes die. Not slaughtered alone in their palace while their city burns to the ground and their people are murdered in the street like beggars and dogs.

Just then the door split further, metal bars and axes finished the divide. Sheshai stood in front of his throne at the far end of the Great Hall, looking like an indestructible warrior with a large shield and spear at the ready. The men began to pile into the Great Hall through the split door. As they walked in, their shouts died and they stood around in awe of the sheer beauty and magnitude of the room. One of the men who entered first was full of blood. He wore a metal helmet on his head and a metal plate on his chest and held a sword in each hand. He looked down the great foyer to Sheshai. With the awe of the room wearing off of him and his rage returning, he yelled out: "Giant, thou art a combination of everything unholy. The Lord our God has granted us this land. And I am here to claim it."

Sheshai stepped towards the crowd and pointed his spear, "And what is thy name, small man? Tell me, who are the people that slither around under the cover of night like snakes killing defenseless children and women? Who makes claim to land that is not theirs? Who blasphemies the name of Yahweh as if he calls a servant?"

The blooded man stepped closer as the crowd of men behind him still continued to grow larger.

"I am Joshua, son of Nun, descendant of Abraham and we are the Israelites. The Lord God's chosen people."

Sheshai, knowing the end of his life was moments away, finally understood his grandfather. To fall alone didn't mean to stand alone; he meant a warrior *falls* in battle.

He raised his spear toward heaven and in a loud thunderous voice said, "I Sheshai, son of Anak, son of Arba, son of the Elohim curse thou Joshua. For thou art a people who expand thy kingdom with a sword, under war and death. I curse thy son's that while they remain on land that is not theirs, they will never know peace."

With that, the Archangel Uriel pulled out his sword, extended his arm and lowered the tip to the floor. A brilliant blast of light exploded where the tip had touched and flooded the Great Hall momentarily blinding everyone. When the light faded Uriel was gone. The men behind Joshua were startled by the flash; some began murmuring about being cursed, while others whispered they should leave. Joshua sensed he was rapidly losing his men. "Did thou see men? Yahweh, the Lord our God was here before us. He claimed this to be our land. Thou art witnesses to His glory."

Then Joshua charged Sheshai The men behind him had again regained their zest and followed him.

The Nephilim prince, unfamiliar with physical combat, swung the spear in front of him like a club. The tree-sized weapon easily swiped the first three men heavy into the palace wall, and again another three with the returning blow. This was easier than he expected. Perhaps he can still save his kingdom and his family. Perhaps by daylight, the Nephilim can recoup the city's losses. Perhaps he will still die peacefully in his bed... then he felt the bludgeoning chop of an axe on the back of his right leg. Collapsing down to one knee, the men stormed him. Swords, axes and spears violated him in an orgy of metal and blood.

On his back, Sheshai could no longer stop or even slow the frenzy. He was at their mercy and they were granting none of it. Finally, Joshua climbed on top of the giant, slick and painted bright red with the Nephilim's own blood. Sheshai watched helplessly as he was being studied the way a butcher examines a steer before the slaughter. Then, Joshua raised his sword and removed Sheshai's head.

CHAPTER THREE

Present day, Halifax, Nova Scotia

Beep! Beep! Beep!

The clock on the nightstand flashed 5:05 A.M. as the alarm pierced the morning calm. Vivica Papp, a thirty-five year old geology professor at Dalhousie University, reached over and clumsily slapped at the clock.

"Getting up? It's your turn to take Charlie to daycare."

Curtis, her husband, rubbed his eyes, letting an unwelcomed dream of ghosts and a haunted house from his childhood slip away. "Yeah, I'm up. And today is your day to sleep in right?"

A groggy 'mmph' was the only reply from the bundle of covers lying beside him. Curtis Papp was a thirty-four year old corporal in the Royal Canadian Air Force. Stationed in 12 Wing Shearwater, the Sea King helicopter base for Canada's East Coast Navy, Curtis was employed as a communication technician, repairing and maintaining everything from computer networks to satellite telephones.

These early mornings can really ruin a day, by 10 am I'm already tired, Curtis thought to himself. Curtis opened his eyes and their cat Sphinx was sitting at the foot of the bed staring at him.

"What? Hungry?" Curtis asked the small cat. Two months earlier the Papp's picked the little kitten up at the SPCA. He had a black and white coat and his face had a confusing design that was similar to a Rorschach ink blot. It resembled the "candlestick/two faces" picture. If it wasn't for the big round eyes, it would be hard to tell you were even looking at his face.

After pulling on a t-shirt and pajama bottoms, Curtis made his way downstairs to turn on the coffee pot. His thoughts thankfully shifted from his shitty dream to the documentary he watched the night before. It was about the divine language of the ancient Egyptians called Hieroglyphics. Egyptian grammar is broken down into three historical levels: Ancient, Classical, and New (many scholars debate whether Coptic script is a fourth Egyptian language or just a Greek hybrid). As the Egyptians evolved so did their language and writings. Hieroglyphics evolved to Hieratic and then further to Demotic. And it was this Demotic writing, actually only a few words of it, that really stuck in his head: *Heaven, angel, man.*

While the coffee was brewing, Curtis did his unofficial morning routine of stretches and back twists. At five feet, ten inches and 175 pounds, he wasn't a big guy — not even one of the bigger guys in his department, but he kept himself in shape.

He gave his back another twist each way (once more to the right and again to the left), trying to readjust whatever the bed popped-out (or popped-in) throughout the night. During a brief tour in Afghanistan in 2004, a suicide bomber blew up himself and the car he was driving at a roadside check point. The blast killed his good friend Ryan, and nearly killed him (Curtis was saved when he reached down to pick up a tool out of his toolbox. The blast was deflected by the cement barriers. Although Curtis missed the initial explosion and flying debris, the force still tossed him like a doll, rewarding him with a concussion and a few broken ribs). Nowadays, his back almost always hurt first thing in the morning and his right foot falls asleep when he sits for too long.

He lumbered up stairs to the toilet to begin his other morning routine feeling like an old man.

"Daddy-is it time to get up yet?" called a little voice from the room next to the bathroom. Charlie is Vivica and Curtis's four year old daughter.

Curtis stopped shaving. With most of his face still covered in white cream, he peered around the door frame. Charlie's big, beautiful green eyes were staring back at him.

"Good morning. You still had twenty minutes to sleep. Let me finish shaving and I will come and get you."

A few minutes later Charlie was enjoying a slow pony ride down the stairs on Curtis's back. He plopped her down at the table with a bowl of Rice Krispies and sliced bananas while *Sponge Bob Square Pants* was playing on the T.V. With his second cup of coffee circulating through his system, Curtis began to feel a little more alive.

An hour later they were both walking to the car, Charlie holding her *Dora the Explorer* back pack and Curtis wearing his green CADPAT uniform and blue Air Force beret. CADPAT, or *Canadian Disruptive Pattern,* is a computer-generated, digital camouflage pattern developed by the Canadian military.

Recently Curtis was moved to the satellite and communications lab. He enjoyed working in 'The Lab' as they called it. It was air conditioned and far more relaxed than the I.T. shop.

"Let's see if you can do your own seatbelt this morning."

"Okay daddy."

After much grunting and groaning and her tongue slightly hanging out of her mouth, she smiled a wide smile when she heard the rewarding "click" sound of the seatbelt tying together.

"I did it! I did it!" she exclaimed in triumph.

"Yes you did. You are my big girl now." Curtis leaned down and gave his daughter a kiss on the forehead, like he does every day when she crawls into her car seat.

"Pretty soon you'll have to get a job. Help us pay some of your bills."

"Daddy!" she responded smiling up at him.

Sitting down behind the wheel he pulled out of the driveway and headed towards the Bumble Bee daycare.

"Do you want to hear my new song daddy?" About every other day Charlie sings a new song from the backseat. The songs are always in Christmas form and fashion and, perhaps more accurately, they are all the same song with just a slight alteration on the lyrics.

> *Christmas is my favourite time*
> *With Christmas trees and presents*
> *I love Santa Claus and Mommy and Daddy.....*

Curtis loved to hear her sing. At least she wasn't shy like he was at her age.

Curtis gave Charlie another kiss before giving her over to Mira, a very large but very kind hearted veteran of the Bumble Bee daycare.

"See you after work Peanut," he said to Charlie as he watched her run over and sat down next to a little blonde girl at a small round table. Smiling to himself, Curtis then headed off to work.

Curtis swiped his ID card and entered the building. He worked within the Headquarters building, which was affectionately referred to by everyone at the Wing as the "Chiclet" building because it resembled several pieces of

Cadbury's Chiclets gum stuck together. Once in the two sets of doors there is a large round foyer. The curved walls have pictures of the Governor General, the current Wing Commander and Executive staff. Doors lead off in all directions to offices and cubicles, many of which Curtis wasn't sure who did what. Taking the spiral stares down to the first level, Curtis walked to the Lab where he worked. Swiping his card again, he entered the restricted area full of equipment used in encryption and decryption of video and data messaging. It had three large benches that formed a horseshoe along the outer walls. With several oscilloscopes, Fluke meters and soldering irons at every station. Curtis walked over to his station and turned on his power bar to warm up his equipment. The fume hood just above the soldering iron automatically came to life and his two Iwatsu TS-81000 Digital/Analog oscilloscopes flashed up their displays and performed a little ballet with blinking LEDs and beeped, stating it was performing a self-tuning diagnostic.

"Corporal Papp, how is the VSAT coming?"

VSAT stands for Very Small Aperture Terminal. It is used extensively for communicating both voice and data in remote areas via satellite.

Curtis turned around to see Sergeant O'Connell standing behind him holding a stainless steel travel mug full of coffee. Sergeant Terrance O'Connell or simply "Sarge" as everyone in the shop called him, was the one sergeant Curtis respected most, and since his department had yet to replace the Master Corporal that recently retired, Sarge was directly in Curtis's chain of command.

"I am just about finished. I had to replace the power cord. On that last deployment, someone in a Humvee ran over the cable, pulled it right out of Stream 1's power supply."

Sergeant O'Connell looked down at the white box. "Good, because we're sending you off out of the country for a few days."

A surprised looked popped on Curtis's face. A sense of adventure and excitement quickly began to rise in him. "Oh, really? To where?"

"To Israel. You should be getting a message in your email from the OC any minute. It should only be for a couple of days, five at the most."

Curtis was beside himself. From experience he had come to realize that the military often makes requests for personnel at the last minute. He has always been the spontaneous type so it has never been an issue.

"What will I be doing there?"

Sarge walked around to the first station and sat down in the chair putting his coffee cup down on the rubber anti-static matting.

"You will read it all in the message, but... you will be setting up communications for the JTF2 unit who will be working with the Israel Defense Force (IDF) in an exercise. It is the first time Canada and Israel have ever correlated an exercise like this."

Curtis turned around and walked to his computer. "Wow! I gotta say I didn't expect anything like this when I woke up this morning. What kind of exercise?"

"You will read it in your message."

Logging onto his computer, Curtis checked his inbox for anything new. Sure enough, at the top of the list, there was an email from Major Dodds, Curtis's commanding officer.

Sarge, watching Curtis's face, took a sip of his coffee. "Well, is it in yet?"

"Yep, right here. It says there will be a briefing later today in Halifax, at the CFB Dockyard, building D201, at 1300 hrs, right after lunch."

Sarge stood up and began walking towards the door. "You know this is a big deal, there is going to be a lot of brass involved. It's quite the opportunity; it could really set off your career."

"Plus it will get me out of this dungeon for a few days. Maybe catch a tan. Israel should be pretty nice this time of year." Curtis said as he began to print out the message.

"Hey Papp, you have my home and BlackBerry numbers right?"

"Ah, yes I have them right here on my desk Sarge."

"Good, give them to Vivica just in case she needs anything. If the car blows a tire and she needs to get to work we'll help her out. Whatever it is, it doesn't matter. Our section looks out for each other."

Curtis looked up at his Sergeant and felt truly touched by the sentiment. One thing he liked about the Air Force is that they *really* do look out for each other. He had never heard any stories of Army Sergeants being sympathetic to their men and he had seen far too often how the Navy "eats their own."

"Thanks Sarge."

Sergeant O'Connell left the room and Curtis looked down at his message.

Now for the really hard part: telling Vivica.

Right after lunch Curtis drove through Dartmouth and over the Angus L. MacDonald Bridge into Halifax. The bridge was built right above the Royal Canadian Navy's dockyard. Curtis made a sharp right turn off the bridge and headed straight into the CFB Dockyard. He showed his ID to the security guards posted at the Admiral's Gate. The old security guard was shadowed by a well-armed soldier in a black combat uniform. He was sporting a C7 automatic and a 'don't test me' scowl on his face. They asked where he was going and how long he would be. Finally, they gave him a pass to stick into his front windshield. The young soldier hit a red button with the flesh of his fist and the gate arm rose, allowing Curtis to enter.

That was unusual, Curtis remarked to himself.

Finding a parking spot in the dockyard was impossible at

the best of times. What this place needed was a multi-level parking garage. Instead, what they had was a parking lot that had the capacity to hold about one third of its employees. Fortunately, he was going to D201, the Maritime Forces Atlantic Headquarters of Canada's East Coast Navy and Intelligence Centre. Because it is located farther away from the actual naval ship yard, there always seemed to be parking. Sure enough, as soon as Curtis pulled into the segregated parking lot a car was pulling out.

Attempting his best impression of The Simpsons' Mr. Burns, Curtis put his finger tips together, *"Excellent."*

Walking into the red-bricked building usually required a salute or two but today the officer traffic was quite a bit higher. It wasn't hard to tell there was something going on today.

As Curtis entered the headquarters he was again greeted by security. Curtis showed the guard his ID, signed the book and put on his visitors pass.

"I am looking for Conference Room 2."

The guard re-examined Curtis. Looking him up and down and deciding he was not a security threat motioned towards a large vault door to his right.

"You need to go through that security door. Do you not have the code?"

"Code?" Curtis patted his uniform pockets and pulled out his printed email message.

The guard furrowed his brow and frustration began to form on his face. "Corporal, that is a secured area, you need a security code to get into the vault. You just can't walk in. Who were you supposed to meet here?"

Curtis opened his paper.

"Well, Major Dodds from Shearwater..." Curtis's eyes spotted the four digit security code that would let him in the vault. "Ha! Found it. So it's just in there?" Curtis said pointing at the metal door.

"Not exactly," the security guard said as he exhaled. At that moment two Petty Officers wearing their "salt and pepper" uniforms and white peaked caps walked in from outside and passed Curtis, walked around a large model display of the Navy's Atlantic fleet and straight to the vault door. The security guard, seeing a way out of having to leave his chair and guide the corporal to his conference room, called to the Petty Officers.

"Excuse me Petty Officer Hahn."

The sailor turned around just before he typed his security code in. "Yes?"

"Could you be so kind and show Corporal Papp here where Conference Room 2 is?"

"Certainly, follow us."

Curtis took a couple of steps with the sailors when the guard leaned forward into his desk and called after him.

"Corporal, corporal, you need to hand in your cell phone up here at the desk, first. No phones allowed inside the shield."

"That's okay," Curtis smiled. "I don't have one."

What? That's a first, the security guard said to himself and watched Curtis walk over to the sailors.

The Petty Officer typed his four digit security code into the number pad just left of the handle on the door. A solid chunking sound and a thud came from within the door. The door popped open two centimeters and the sailor grabbed the handle and pulled the heavy duty door slowly open. The door easily weighed a ton and along the inside centre of the door were copper fingers curled into it. The door opened to a smaller room that held no more than six people. On the other side of the chamber was another large metal door. Curtis had a curious look on his face as he looked at the copper curls along the door. The second petty officer noticed his expression.

"It's to prevent electronic emission from escaping the

vault. See the sign?" The petty officer was pointing to a laminated photocopy of a cell phone within a red circle and a red bar crossing it out.

"That means no cell phones or transmitting devices within these walls. Not that they would work. The vault is a complete shield. It's an emissions security zone or EMSEC Zone."

When the first door was completely closed Curtis got a quick sinking feeling of being trapped, not that he was claustrophobic by any means, but he had never been in situation like this before. Looking around he saw the black bubble of the video camera in the ceiling corner. As he heard the door seal behind him, a small red lamp on the wall in front of him turned green. Petty Officer Hahn pressed a large button beside the lamp and the second door produced the same chunking sound and popped open slightly.

Curtis and the two petty officers stepped out into a hallway. This was not what Curtis expected at all. He thought it would have led directly to the conference room, but instead it looked like an average office space. The hallway carried on directly in front of him leading to the men's and women's washrooms, a water fountain and Conference Room #1. It also spread out to his right and left, with four or five office doors connecting off of it. Many of the doors had additional keypads of their own.

Wow this place is secure, Curtis thought to himself.

"The door with the large #2 hanging above it is your conference room," the other petty officer directed.

"Thank you!" Curtis replied a little intimidated by all the security. As he approached the door he spotted more black bubbles on the ceiling. He could hear talking inside the room and found the door was propped open. As he entered the room, he expected to see a large oval table surrounded by chairs. Instead Curtis found himself standing at the top of a room looking down into a theatre, eight rows high and with fifteen seats in each row. The stage floor area had a polished wooden banister separating itself from the first row of seats. There was an opening at each end leading to a stairway; the second stairway on the opposite side of the room led out to a second exit out of the conference room. There was a podium setup on the far right where the speaker conducts his or her briefs. And on the back wall was a large IMAX-like screen. Directly opposite the screen and to Curtis's immediate right was the control room for the projector and sound system.

So far Curtis counted nineteen people in the room. Three Colonels and a Lieutenant-Colonel were talking together down by the banister. Another six men in grey uniforms with maroon berets folded under their left epaulette were sitting together in far right row, obviously from a foreign military; Curtis had never seen their uniforms before. A woman wearing a smart business suit in her mid-fifties was at the podium working on her laptop, making what Curtis guessed to be last minute adjustments to her presentation. He decided to play it safe and sit in the first seat of the top row, close to the exit.

The remaining people didn't sport the classic military look at all. Their hair was longer than normal and they were wearing casual clothes, some in khaki pants or expensive blue jeans, collared shirts and nice sweaters. You could tell by their impressive physique and overall air about them they were professional and dangerous. Curtis assumed they were the JTF 2 team.

Joint Task Force 2 or JTF 2 is Canada's elite counter-terrorism team. It is labeled a joint task force because it is comprised of the very best members of all three elements of Canada's military: Navy, Army and Air Force. Created on April 1st, 1993, they employ both assaulters and supporters. The *assaulters* are the highly trained commandos that bust into the homes, buildings and complexes of their enemies and "eliminate" the target. The *supports* are the people who help them get the job done like pilots, medical staff and radar technicians.

More people filed into the room and fill up the seats around Curtis. He noticed his Commanding Officer Major Dodds walking down the far set of stairs to greet the brass at the bottom. Shaking hands with the other officers and saying something apparently witty, Dodds looked around and noticed Curtis. He gave him a nod and then laughed hardily at something funny one of the Colonels said.

Curtis liked his CO enough but he didn't really know him very well. He just watched and thought how phony military officers could be. It seemed to him that half of their time was used greasing the wheels for promotion or networking for promotions. In his ten years of military service, Curtis had felt the strong divide between the commissioned and the non-commissioned ranks, and even held a slight prejudice for their better pensions, but he had to admit he never wanted those bars on his epaulette.

Within a few minutes the room was full. Exactly at 1 p.m., the lady in the suit approached the banister and asked everyone to take their seats.

"Good afternoon. My name is Lindsey Hilroy. I am the civilian liaison to Lieutenant-General Matthew McAdams and Public Relations Executive for the Canadian Special Operations Forces Command or better known as CANSOFCOM. General McAdams wanted to express to you that he wished he could have been here today but he is at the Dwyer Hill Training Centre in Ottawa with the Minister of Defense going over the very things we are going to talk about. Before we get started I would like to introduce our special guests."

Lindsey gestured to a deeply tanned man sitting in the first row. "This is Major-General Dauer of the Israel Defense Force — Southern Command." A stalky man stood up, turned to the group of people behind him, smiled and nodded and sat back down.

"And to his left is Rabbi Zakovitch." The man sitting next to the general stood up and turned around smiling and waved to everyone. The rabbi wore a similar uniform as the Major-General. He had a strong, broad face and a long white beard.

"Rabbi Zakovitch is the Chief Military Rabbinate; he advises the Chief of General Staff on religious, moral and legal issues facing their troops."

The brief carried on for two more hours, laying out the exercise. In two days time the JTF2 team, along with a communications and support teams, will fly out of Canadian Forces Base Greenwood here in Nova Scotia to Israel's Nevatim Air Force Base. From there the Canadian Task Force will participate in coordinated counter-terrorism training scenarios with the Israel Defense Force. The techniques and experience the IDF has developed over the years, plus the environment and terrain will make the training invaluable. From there the brief was filled in with a lot of "ground breaking" this, "good for both countries" that, full of political motivation and a lot of back slapping.

Curtis had been around long enough to know that militaries are used as political pawns. *No doubt within the next year there will be some kind of trade negotiations,* he thought to himself. It didn't matter to him either way. He was paid well to do what the government wanted, and if they wanted to send him to Israel for five days, no complaints there.

"The Rabbi will also be briefing us on some cultural differences and what to expect. Remember, while you are in Israel you will be representing the Canadian government and Canada as a whole, whether you are wearing a uniform or not. Do not get caught up in Israeli-Palestinian politics. If questioned by the media, you have no comment and you can direct them to me or Captain Bell, our Public Relations officer for this exercise. It will only be for a few days and we are not expecting any problems. Are there any questions?"

A hand went up in front of Curtis a few rows down. It belonged to a young sergeant he had seen around the wing. Sgt. Kraft was wearing his CADPAT uniform, as were only a small handful of people in the group, including Curtis.

"Yes Sergeant?"

"Sergeant Kraft, Ma'am. You had briefed that this exercise has been in the making for almost a year. And I just received my message for deployment on Friday. Now, I am ready to go, but I know there are a few people here who just received their messages today. I was just hoping maybe you could clear something up for them: why are our support members being requested at the last minute? Thank you."

Wow, thought Curtis. *That sergeant just called everyone in Ottawa who is involved with this exercise careless with respect to time management as well as to the personnel on the ground in front of many of those same people and the Israeli guests.*

Sgt. Kraft didn't seem to notice or perhaps just didn't care that all of the officers in the front row and throughout the conference room were staring directly at him — or perhaps *through* him. One of the Colonels leaned over to another Colonel, said something and nodded. Even Curtis thought the question was, given the present audience, in extreme poor taste. He even felt embarrassed for Lindsey for being put on the spot like that, although he was wondering the same question.

Lindsey's face turned a little flush, but as a veteran bureaucrat she quickly composed herself.

"Yes, thank you sergeant. I must apologize to those members who found out at the last minute about their involvement in this ground-breaking cooperation. As I am sure we can all appreciate, our own Defense Minister McDonald has been working on this collaboration with the Israeli Defense Minister for sometime in secret, to dot the *I*s and cross the *T*s. Unfortunately, because it is our two nations' first international military exercise, when the okay was finally given, the window of opportunity to have this exercise was very narrow. But with the professionalism of the Canadian Forces and the Israel Defense Force we were able to make it a go. Thank you, sergeant for your personal sacrifices and a very good question."

"Holy shit! She shut him up pretty good," whispered a stranger sitting next to Curtis. Curtis never noticed this man sitting there before and was a little startled. He was wearing civilian clothes and didn't really look like a military member. He had a briefcase next to him with a small digital recorder sitting on his arm rest and he was writing quick remarks onto a note pad. Curtis noticed his ID badge around his neck: "The Royal Canadian Air Force Journal - Eavery Parker."

It took a few minutes but other people started to ask questions. Curtis looked back at the reporter.

"I'm surprised they let you in here."

"Oh no, they *wanted* this covered. It's a big deal. I was lucky enough to beat out the Maple Leaf and the Army Journal. I've been covering the JTF for some time now so I guess it bought me some access."

The reporter held out his hand, "Eavery."

Curtis shook it and introduced himself. "Are you coming to Israel?"

"Oh yeah! I will be flying out with you guys from Greenwood. What is it that you do?"

"I'm a comms tech, but I am not too sure why I was selected," Curtis explained.

Lindsey Hilroy asked the group if there were any more questions. Curtis raised his hand.

"Yes at the top, go ahead."

"Good day Ma'am, Corporal Papp. I am a communications technician with 12 Wing Shearwater. I don't mean to seem ignorant of the situation but I am not sure why the JTF2 — with their highly advanced communication systems would require any *outside* help."

"Very good question, Corporal Papp," Lindsey replied.

Major Dodds stood up. "Maybe I could answer that Ms Hilroy. Lateral technology is the short answer. Corporal Papp, you are correct, that the JTF 2 has their own unique communications network, with specialized receiver/transceivers developed specifically for them. And that is the problem we are solving here. Their systems are not compatible with the Israeli systems. So we are utilizing our common technology, and as a technician with this equipment, your services are also being utilized. We will be employing our high frequency radio, the QRT or the Quick Reaction Terminal for *field-to-FOB* communications and the VSAT system so we can send voice and data, not to forget live video feed from the drones flying over head, via satellite from the Forward Operating Base to Ottawa and Jerusalem."

Lindsey took a step closer to the banister. "Where our respective ministries will be able to *scrutinize,* for lack of a better word, the exercise."

"Not too harshly, I hope," one of the colonels interjected. Some people in the group chuckled at the comment, but everyone knew with this event that "scrutinize" was the perfect description of what the generals in Ottawa were going to do.

"Does that answer your question, Corporal Papp?" Maj Dodds asked, not actually caring for his reply but expecting it to be, "Yes, Sir, it did. Thank you."

True to his expectation, Curtis replied. Dodds, feeling good with himself for contributing to this high profile yet casual briefing, sat down.

Curtis leaned over to the reporter. "Well Eavery, now we

know what I'll be doing." Eavery chuckled to himself and scribbled something onto his note pad.

After the brief, Curtis picked up Charlie at the daycare and stopped off at the Value Grocer, the small Eastern Passage grocery store.

"Want me to BBQ steaks for supper tonight?"

"Sure!" Charlie replied galloping her *My Little Pony* doll across some pre-packaged cobs of corn.

"Let's grab some of those big potatoes and some asparagus too." He was going to need some kissing up tonight before he told Vivica his newly developed travel agenda.

And maybe some wine.

Back at the house, as Vivica pulled into the driveway she could smell the BBQ. Curtis was sitting in a deck chair in front of the garage holding a glass of red wine. Stepping out of the car, she smiled as she approached him.

"Well don't you look comfortable," said Vivica. "Red wine? I hope you have some for me, I could use it."

"Oh, yeah! There is a full bottle of Jost cooling in the fridge."

Charlie came screaming around the corner from the back yard. "Mommy!" she jumped up into Vivica's arms almost knocking her over.

Vivica was trying to hold onto her while Charlie smothered her face with kisses.

"Charlie! Charlie! You are getting too big for mommy to hold you," she said putting Charlie down and kneeling in front of her. "Did you have fun today at school?"

"Yes. I drew you some pictures. Come in the house; I will show you." Grabbing her mother's hand, Charlie dragged her into the house.

Curtis took another sip of wine and laughed to himself.

The five days in Israel are going to be exciting, but he is going to miss being home.

Later that evening, after she had her bath and two bedtime stories, Charlie was finally asleep. Curtis and Vivica were relaxing on the couch. Being the parents of a four year old, this was the only quiet time they had together. He poured the last drop of the red wine into her glass.

"So steak, red wine... once you begin massaging my feet I know you're up to something."

"What? You think I am that predictable?" Curtis tried to counter.

"What is it?" Vivica probed.

Curtis filled her in on the day's events, and began massaging her feet.

"So you bought a bottle of wine to tell me you are heading out for five days?" Vivica asked.

"No. I cooked porterhouse to *tell* you I was leaving for five days. I bought the bottle of wine because I know what wine *does* to you... and I am leaving in two days."

"Curtis Papp, you dirty man. You would take full advantage of a woman under the influence?"

"How do you think we got Charlie?" Curtis said and then laughed out loud. Shaking her head, Vivica smiled and slapped him in the arm.

"And I don't think you are under that much influence right now."

"No," she replied, "too bad for you."

"Really? Because I have another bottle in the fridge."

This time Vivica laughed out loud.

When Curtis walked into the lab the next morning, his head hurt and he was waiting for the Advil to kick in.

Sarge had left an email telling him that his equipment had been packed up by Granier and Robertson; two other corporals in Curtis's department, and sent ahead to Greenwood. He told Curtis that once he was done with his paperwork (claims, immunization, passport, etc.) he could go home and spend the remainder of the day packing and getting ready. The shuttle to Greenwood is leaving Shearwater at 0300 hrs. *Don't miss it!*

Nevatim Air Force Base, Israel

The Nevatim Israeli Air Force Base (28) was built in 1947 and modernized in 1983 with help from the U.S. Government. It is one of eleven points in the Negev region and the strategic stronghold for the Southern Command. It is home to the Golden Eagles, the 140 Squadron of F-16A/B fighter jets. The airbase had two main runways traveling east-west and four taxiways leading to the hangers that held their F16s, and CC130 Hercules transport planes.

Stepping off the CC-150 Polaris transport plane onto the tarmac, Curtis felt a blast of dry, hot air that had swept across the ancient desert. He left Nova Scotia at 6 a.m. and touched down in Israel just before midnight. Although the flight was comfortable enough, and he had taken several naps, Curtis was looking forward to stretching out. It may be midnight here, but back home it was around 4:30 pm and some authentic cuisine sounded pretty tempting. Being a military airbase, the aircraft did not have the luxury of an elevated walkway so all the personnel had to exit down a long flight of stairs. Everyone gathered at the bottom of the stairway waiting for their luggage and be given direction on where to go next.

Curtis looked around. It may have been midnight, but the entire airbase was lit up and Curtis could see only a barren landscape for about a kilometer. There was a sweet fragrance floating on the air — something Curtis didn't expect at all from a desert.

"Oh, I've missed that smell," Eavery said as he walked up to Curtis.

"That smells so fresh; what is it?" Curtis asked.

"You can't see them from the tarmac, but there are fields of wild red poppies and yellow daisies just painting the rolling wadi-side," Eavery added, then continued. "The Negev desert, which surrounds the airbase, is a very unique desert. It receives moisture from the Mediterranean. It doesn't have the trees like, say, in New Brunswick, but it's not a desert like the Sahara; it more resembles the badlands of Alberta."

Taking a deep breath, Curtis was already impressed with Israel. "The pictures in the brief showed rolling hills of dried bushes and tumble weeds, I wasn't thinking fields of flowers."

"Yeah, we'll be deeper into the desert for the exercise, further out to the northeast. This area here is beautiful, and big on ecotourism. The little village just down the road, Nevatim, has about one thousand people living there and most are organic farmers. It's a Moshav — a kind of cooperative agricultural community; they grow everything from potatoes and tomatoes to wheat."

"Wow!" Curtis said. "I had no idea."

Two large vans pulled up beside the group. A young female captain stepped out and briskly walked over to Colonel Nestlie, the only one in the group who was in uniform. The captain, wearing the brown uniform of the Israeli Air Force, came to attention and saluted the colonel. She explained that she was going to take the officers and civilians to the officer's sleeping quarters as soon as he was ready, and that the second van driven by the Israeli Military Police was going to take the sergeants and below to the enlisted sleeping quarters. Curtis couldn't help think that the officer's quarters were going to be considerably nicer than the one he was going to be staying in.

It wasn't long before they had their luggage and were

ready to head off to their accommodations. Colonel Nestlie stepped up onto the second step of the staircase.

"Excuse me, everyone. It is very late here in Israel and our jet lag will render us pretty useless tomorrow. That means you have tomorrow to recoup yourself. Personally, I plan on hitting the local links and getting at least eighteen holes in by noon. I understand the village on Nevatim is near by and has excellent kosher desserts. To each your own, I will see you at 0500 hrs on Sunday morning."

Smiles and hoots spread throughout the group. Their equipment would be handled by airbase staff and secured until they were ready for it sometime in the next few days.

When Curtis was given the key to his room, he immediately noticed it was an electronic key similar to the kind of key one would get from the front desk of a Best Western.

Promising, Curtis thought to himself. Perhaps he won't have to share his room with two or three other people like he expected, and like he has done countless times at Canadian bases and abroad. When he entered his room it was more like a motel room than a military barracks. The room was small but cozy and fully furnished. He had a private bathroom to himself, a double bed already fully made, a couch, a TV, a microwave, a small fridge, and a desk with internet connections. This was going to be awesome. Curtis was used to a room that had two or four rusty, stained single mattresses, and bed sheets folded in the closet with a scratchy, grey wool fire blanket for warmth (which was anything but). Yes, to Curtis, this was the Hilton in one of the most ancient regions in the world.

At first light I am going into town, Curtis thought to himself. *Now what to do until then?*

Curtis wasn't tired but the base was closed down for the night, and he sure as hell wasn't wandering the perimeter.

He propped the pillows up on the bed, turned on the T.V., and began to surf the channels. Surprisingly, many of the channels were in English. Within minutes the day's stress and excitement got the better of him and the last thing Curtis heard before falling asleep was an info-mercial: *Vince was going to make America skinny again, one slap at a time.*

7 a.m. came pretty quick; very groggily, Curtis pulled himself out of bed and climbed into the shower. Rubbing his face, he decided to shave later. After sorting through his duffle bag, Curtis put on a wrinkled pair of shorts, a collared shirt and sandals, and headed downstairs to the main entrance of the barracks. There was a rounded front desk manned by an airman.

"Good morning," Curtis greeted the private. "I am looking to go into town for a while. Is there a duty vehicle or taxi I can get a ride with?"

The private looked up at Curtis a little startled and surprised.

"You want to go into Nevatim? There isn't anything there. It's a village of a couple hundred people, mostly farmers," the airman replied in a strong Israeli accent.

"Oh, I would like to look around. Maybe get some authentic kosher cuisine before I start into the field rations."

The private finished his comment on his Facebook page and folded his laptop and stood up. Grabbing some keys from a metal key box behind the desk he said, "I can take you. I need to stretch my legs anyways."

"Fantastic!" Curtis extended his hand and introduced himself.

"My name is David Chodosh. Welcome to Israel," the airman replied.

The "duty vehicle" was a silver Mercedes-Benz C-Class sedan. Curtis chuckled to himself thinking about the Chrysler Sebring they drive around base back in Canada. Driving out the front gate and down a paved solitary road for about eight kilometers, Curtis could see the countryside much more easily now. At the far end of his scope, he could see the beginning of the badlands, the rolling hills or wadis. But as the road took him more southwest he was amazed at all the colour, the abundant greens, reds and whites of the local flowers. They turned right onto highway 25, an impressive four lane highway that travels from Natal Oz at the edge of the Gaza Strip to highway 90 near Jordan. Within a few minutes they pulled into the small village of Nevatim. The streets were lined with palm trees and a fair amount of houses. A hospital and a nursing home greeted them as they came off the highway. The downtown core was tiny with a few shops, a market, and a synagogue. The Mercedes-Benz pulled up to a coffee shop; on one side of the shop was the Cochin Heritage Center and on the other was Nevatim Secretariat. Across the street was the HaMeyasdim Gardens.

Curtis looked around the town.

"See, not much here. But this is the best coffee in town," David chuckled. "It would have to be, it's the only one."

Curtis looked up at the sign; it was written in both Hebrew and Arabic and he couldn't read one word. David could tell he had no idea what it said.

"It's the 'ale álp'; you should try the borekas."

"Thanks." Curtis got out of the car and closed the door. The window rolled down and the private leaned across the passenger seat. "Do you have a way back?"

Curtis bent over. "Not yet."

David scribbled some numbers on the back of a gas receipt. "Here, this is the phone number to the front desk. We always keep it manned, except for right now, of course. When you're ready to go, I am sure it would be no problem to come and get you."

"Thank you very much."

David waved to him. "Shalom."

Curtis waved back as the Mercedes drove off. Turning around, he looked at the humble coffee shop. It didn't appear to be any different than the "mom and pop" greasy spoons across North America. The morning was already starting to get hot and the door was propped open so Curtis walked in. There were six empty tables in the lobby and no owner in site. Since no one saw him walk in, Curtis wasn't sure if he should sit down at a table or look for a bell to ring.

Would ringing a bell be rude? What about a nonchalant cough or a light hello? Curtis decided to sit down at a table, and as he moved his chair across the floor he got a dragging sound that alerted the waiter in the kitchen.

A plump young man in his mid-twenties approached Curtis. He had a round face, a small beard and black rimmed glasses.

"Boker tov! Good morning."

Feeling a little sheepish, Curtis returned the greeting.

"What can I get for you this morning?"

Curtis looked up with an expression of uncertainty and confusion. This was not the accent that he had expected, the waiter sounded like a New Yorker.

Curtis pulled a menu from the center of the table. "I would like a coffee to start."

The waiter nodded and walked back behind the counter. The menu only consisted of one page folded in half. The pictures to help identify the selection were in black and white, obviously done on a home printer. Not being able to read anything on the menu, with the pictures only causing more discomfort, Curtis folded the menu back up and replaced it in the center. The waiter placed the coffee in front of Curtis with a tube of sugar and a spoon. Looking down, Curtis was surprised to see that his coffee cup was a small demitasse; the type of cup usually used to serve espresso. He should have known: throughout his career, Curtis had travelled around the world and within many eastern countries he noticed that people drank their coffee and tea in these small cups.

"Can I get you something from the kitchen?"

"Yes, I heard your *borekas* are really good, I'll try some of them."

"The best in town! We have several types." The waiter reached down and opened the menu in front of Curtis, pointing to a small picture of a pastry at the bottom of the page that looked like an apple strudel.

"We have some filled with spinach and cheese, or ground beef, liver, or our breakfast borekas have egg and cheddar."

Curtis felt his stomach growl; this was what he was waiting for. "I'll try a couple of the egg and cheddar."

The waiter looked over at him, "I will bring just one to start, they're pretty big — it fills a plate."

Curtis nodded and the waiter headed back towards the kitchen. He took a sip of his coffee and looked up at the waiter who was keeping himself busy behind the counter.

Curtis eyed him for a minute. "Excuse me, I don't mean to pry but your accent — are you from New York?"

The waiter looked up at Curtis and then continued his work. "Yes, I was. My grandparents were from Poland, and prior to World War II they moved to New York. And now, fulfilling Jeremiah's prophecy, I call Israel home. And you, you must be Canadian? Flew in last night?"

The question took Curtis by surprised. Most people outside of Canada assumed he was an American, especially Americans.

"Yes, how did you know that?"

"It's a small town; everyone knows everything that goes on around here."

"I know what you mean," Curtis said thinking back to the small town he grew up in.

After a couple of minutes a ding from the cook's bell echoed from the kitchen. The waiter walked over with his borekas and a pot of coffee to refill his cup. Looking down at his plate, Curtis was glad he only ordered one; the borekas filled the plate almost entirely. It was very similar to a Cornish pasty without the pinched ridge on the one side. By this time Curtis felt famished and he cut the pastry in half watching the cheese, egg and spinach firmly stay in place. It was one of the best dishes he had tasted in months. It reminded him of the meals he ate in Turkey on another outing paid for by the military. It wasn't long before he finished his breakfast and the coffee had him vibrating. Walking up to the counter he paid the waiter in American currency.

"Is there a bus that goes up to Hebron?"

"Hebron? No! But sometimes my cousin Zachariah drives up there for fresh lamb; he might give you a ride. When he comes in I can ask him if you like?"

Curtis smiled at his good fortune. "That would be great. Does he come by in the mornings?"

"Yeah, probably in an hour or so."

"I will be back in an hour then," Curtis said triumphantly, feeling that his day was turning out far better than he thought it would.

Walking the breakfast off, Curtis toured through the town. He watched a small curio shop open up ahead of him. The window displayed colourful tea pots, Turkish hookahs and ancient-looking artifacts. *A good place to waste some time*, Curtis thought, and walked in.

"Shalom," called the curator from behind the counter.

"Good morning," Curtis replied.

"Welcome!" the man exclaimed more excitedly and hurried around from the counter towards Curtis. The shop keep was shorter and rounder than Curtis with a balding head and a very hospitable smile. Shaking his hand graciously and welcoming him again he said, "You must be the Canadian?"

"Yes." Curtis said laughing, feeling as if he was the center of some practical joke he was unaware of, waiting for a Jewish Ashton Kutcher to claim he had just been *Punk'd*.

"How did you know?"

"Small town," the friendly man said. "Please come in; look around. Would you like some coffee or tea?"

"No, thank you, I just had some down the street."

"Oh, at 'ale álp,' best coffee in town! Very good! Did you try the borekas? The liver is my favourite."

A combination of the man's energy and the caffeine from breakfast put a large smile on Curtis's face and he couldn't help but chuckle aloud.

"Yes I did. It was very delicious and filling."

"Please look around, tell me what you like; I will make you a good deal."

Curtis walked up and down isles of glass shelving that contained ceramic vases depicting the exodus out of Egypt, silver menorahs, a pewter Star of David, hookahs, marble chest sets, jars of water claiming to be from the Dead Sea, and bottles of sand with labels on it saying, *"From the sands of Babylon."*

As Curtis walked through the aisles, the shopkeeper kept on talking to him from his stool behind the counter.

"Canada. Very nice place. Cold. My cousin Jacob moved to Canada, Toronto. He says it is a very nice place, but the traffic is very bad, like Jerusalem during the Easter festival. Everybody is in a hurry. That's why I like the country. No hurry, no stress..."

Curtis continued on looking further to the back of the store where he was able to tune him out a little. A small doll carved out of sandstone and not much larger than the palm of his hand caught Curtis's eye. He picked it up and examined it closer. It wasn't particularly well done; most of its features were washed smooth, but there was a faint energy emanating from it. He put it back down on the shelf and picked up a wooden dreidel sitting beside it. Nope, he didn't want the dreidel; he reached back and picked the doll up. A familiarity to it made him think of his family. There was definitely something very pleasant about the carving. Looking around he could swear he could smell fresh baked bread — not bakery fresh but homemade fresh. Curtis found himself lulled into a real sense of calmness, even peacefulness.

"Oh, you like that? Very old. My cousin found that when he was digging sewer lines in Bani Naim," the keeper said from over his shoulder.

Curtis turned to him. "You're allowed to take artifacts from excavation sites?" Curtis asked him a little unsure.

"No, no! Not excavation site, construction site, building sub-division. Running sewer and water lines under ground," the shopkeeper explained.

Curtis was still a little confused.

"But don't you need to tell someone about these finds?"

"Israel is a very old land. Even before God gave us this land, people have been living here for thousands of years. Every time you move some dirt, you find something someone lost. So my cousin found that doll very old. He also found this…"

Pulling a large black rod from the top shelf and holding it firmly in his hand he showed it to Curtis.

"Found it at the site of Gomorrah. You like?"

"What?" Curtis took a step back. "No."

The old man put the rod back on the top shelf. "That's why it's on the top shelf; no one likes."

"I do like this," Curtis said holding out the doll. "I have a buddy back home — his son likes anything ancient. I think he would get a kick out of this."

The shopkeeper quickly took the doll from Curtis and went to get a box to wrap it in. When the artifact left his hand, Curtis felt a little unsettled, as if he forgot something, like calling a friend for his birthday. At the counter Curtis noticed all types of foreign currency displayed on the wall. Among the bills Curtis spied the familiar face of Sandy McTire, the regal looking Scotsman emblazoned on most Canadian Tire money.

Curtis shook his head and pointed at the black and grey $2 bill.

"Did someone actually pay you with that?"

The shopkeeper eyed the certificate and, feeling a little embarrassed for being duped, said, "Yes, many, many years ago. It is okay; I overcharged him for his teapot. But not you, you get very good deal. You pay with Visa, yes?"

Curtis stepped onto the sidewalk with his new souvenir and the early afternoon heat hit him hard. He heard a voice calling from down the street. "Hey! Excuse me! Pal!"

Curtis turned to see a young guy in his twenties jogging over to him. He was wearing a faded American Eagle golf shirt and green khaki cut-off shorts and sandals. He had on a New York Rangers baseball cap with curly dark hair poking out along the bottom.

"You must be the Canadian?" he said and held out his hand.

Curtis shook his hand and noticed he also had a New York accent. "Curtis. And you must be Zachariah?"

"Zack, just Zack. Zachariah is a little too Old Testament for me. I understand you are looking for a ride to Hebron? Well, if you're ready I am leaving in a few minutes."

That suited Curtis perfectly. He had only today to get some sightseeing done, and so far it was going better than expected.

CHAPTER FOUR

Veszprem, Hungary

Gergõ Mátyás stood in the window overlooking the city. The top floor of the Bishop's Palace within the walled section of the Castle gave a splendid view of the red and orange rooftops of the homes and shops that make up the city and the valley off into the distance. The Castle of Veszprém was built on the Bakony Hills within the Balaton Uplands, and sits on one of the seven hills that make up the city. Constructed in the ninth century, the fortress has an encircling wall that confines the cluster of baroque, gothic and Romanesque cathedrals and palaces.

The Bishop's Palace was completed in 1776 and is now the central office of an even more ancient fraternity, the KRÁJCÁR. Looking down over the city that his ancestors built usually gave Gergõ a sense of entitlement as head of both the Society and Brotherhood. The Society or *Társadalom* was the KRÁJCÁR's executive committee while it's Brotherhood or *Testvériség* was its sanctified enforcement, but today's news made the posh palace feel more like a fortress waiting for a battle. Gergõ pulled his focus from the city and looked at his reflection in the glass. Standing at five foot seven inches he wasn't a tall man but he demanded respect; he was bred for it. He ran his fingers through his hair admiring his elongated skull. A true descendant to Attila the Hun, this was his land, not just the city of Veszprém, but all of Hungary. Unfortunately, that is not the direction his life was destined for — at least not yet.

Gergõ sat back down at the head of the large English oak table, and looked up at the grand shield on the wall. He was told from childhood that Attila himself created the KRÁJCÁR *Társadalom* and subsequent *Testvériség* and designed their herald: a golden rampant lion standing on three green hills below two golden stars. The lion represented royalty: *his* birthright. The green hills depicted the great battles won against those unworthy of the *Knowledge,* and the stars were the heavens from where the angel Caviel gave Attila the Sword of God that he used to take down their enemies. After all, Attila was known the world over as *The Scourge of God.*

He rubbed his forearm where a tattoo of the crest had marked his body since his fourth birthday. Bringing himself back to the conversation, Gergõ turned to face the other six. József Söröss continued his briefing.

"That's two more than last month, and a full eight more than this time last year."

"That makes how many in total?" asked Gergõ.

"Nineteen so far," József replied, double checking his figures.

"And the year is only partially complete," remarked Ákos Simon, sitting opposite József at the polished oak table.

Elek Szalai, the KRÁJCÁR's second in command and eldest, straightened himself and pressed his back into the chair. "There has been a steady increase for years, this latest jump seems to suggest something significant is about to take place."

Gergõ has noticed the pattern also. His position will be as it always has been: the same position as his father's and his father's father, all the way back to Attila himself. Rid the world of these abominations.

"We need to kill them all before that can happen."

CHAPTER FIVE

A network of roads that are primarily for Israeli use and which connect Israeli settlements and other infrastructure to each other and to Israel. Palestinian vehicular access into these roads is either restricted or prevented and ultimately diverted. Consequently, these roads have become barriers.

U.N. Office for the Coordination of Humanitarian Affairs CAP 2008

Highway 60, Israel

"So why don't you pick up your meat in Be'er Sheva? It's a lot closer than Hebron," Curtis asked feeling obligated to maintain small talk.

"I have a cousin in Hebron who butchers the lamb and makes it kosher, and a majority of the people in Hebron are Palestinian so he doesn't receive a lot of business," Zack replied. "We're approaching the Green Line. You do have your passport with you, right?"

Curtis was a little uncomfortable by the question. "Yes, I'm carrying my passport, but why would I need it?"

"The Green Line or *Shani Line* is the 1949 Armistice Agreement Line, creating the West Bank and separating

Israeli land from Palestinian land. Just past the town of Meitar is a check point and for about eight kilometers highway 60 becomes restricted."

Curtis was beginning to feel uncomfortable. "Restricted? For who?"

Zack looked over at Curtis. "From the Palestinians, of course. But we shouldn't have a problem."

"That's a relief, but why do you say that?"

"Because we have a yellow license plate and the van is registered to my Jewish cousin."

Curtis could tell he was about to get into the type of conversation he was briefed to strictly avoid.

Zack continued. "There are dozens of highways — called the Apartheid Roads — throughout the West Bank linking Israeli settlements to Israel. Those are called *Israeli-only* roads and there are other roads strictly used by Palestinians called *Palestinian-only* roads. The Palestinian license plates are green and they have to have special permits to use our roads."

This world was completely alien to Curtis. Never in his military career had he even heard of something like this still going on today. It made him think of the black segregation from white-only stores and restaurants.

As they passed Meitar, Curtis could see up ahead what looked like an average border crossing between the United States and Canada. The van slowed down as it approached the checkpoint, the four lane highway filtered through four gates. High speed cameras were mounted above the road to take pictures of the driver, passenger and license plate. On the side of the checkpoint, the Israeli highway patrol was meticulously probing an older model Volvo station wagon. Its four doors and back hatch were open. It was obvious to Curtis that everything that was once inside the car was now on the ground. The driver was in his forties and was holding,

Curtis assumed, his daughter while his wife was placing a blanket over some fresh produce, trying to prevent the sun from spoiling it.

The pit in Curtis's stomach was getting bigger.

What am I doing here? I could easily cause an international incident with such a high profile exercise about to take place. At the very least being held for hours in some checkpoint interrogation room trying to explain myself. What was with this irrational desire to go to Hebron? Hitching rides with some guy I had never even met before, driving through guarded gates and down restricted highways. Who the fuck has an '-only' highway? Zack sitting there could be some kind of Zionist fanatic. There could be anything is the back of this van: M-16s, rocket launchers... Curtis's imagination carried on.

As they crawled up to the border guard, Curtis felt very flushed and very nervous. Zack rolled down the window and raised his hand, "Shalom!"

"Shalom!" the guard answered and waved them through.

"That was it?" Curtis asked still holding his breath.

"Of course," Zack replied. "That was my other cousin Malachi, and you, my friend, do not in any way resemble a Palestinian."

Curtis could feel himself start to relax. That small little panic attack brought him some perspective regarding this side of the world. His curiosity was getting the better of him.

"I don't mean to sound ignorant, but why are the roads segregated?"

"To prevent 'undesirables' from utilizing the infrastructure."

"But doesn't the very nature of the network cause divisions through many towns and regions within the West Bank?"

Zack was firm in his beliefs and didn't like it when outsiders disagreed with them. "They are causing their own economic crisis by launching missiles into our settlements, killing our children and then pointing the finger at Israel. And our roads are segregated so some *Muslim* doesn't drive up and shoot us or blow us off the road. There are thousands of those people around here. Driving up to Hebron or anywhere else in the West Bank would be suicide."

Curtis had entered the very conversation he was told to avoid and could hear the tension begin to increase in Zack's voice. Although he *knew* these were histories of indifference, Curtis just couldn't understand it.

"Well, I suppose you do what you have to. Personally I would just stay out of it," Curtis said hoping that would end a conversation that was becoming quite uncomfortable.

"That's what I like about you Canadians: you always… stay out of it."

Curtis guessed he was probably referring to Rwanda — not exactly a high point in Canadian intervention. But he wondered if Zack had ever heard of Afghanistan?

While lazily scanning the countryside, a flash of light caught Curtis's eye. A half second later a large pop came from Curtis's window as it exploded and shards of glass pummeled the inside of the cab.

Zack jerked and swerved the van inside his lane but was able to maintain enough control to keep it on the road.

"What was that?" Curtis asked, frantically looking around the cab.

"We were just shot at," Zack replied through gritted teeth, anger and adrenaline flooding his system. "My cousin is going to be pissed." He searched the driver's side door and found the hole made by the fired round. He circled and caressed the area with his fingers, feeling the radiant heat of the bullet and the smooth puncture of the metal where the door frame swallowed the slug.

Snapping out of his daze, Zack rapidly dialed the

checkpoint back in Meitar describing in Hebrew the location of the van and approximate location of the shooter.

As the gravity of the situation took hold, Curtis's own adrenaline began to flow as his heart kicked in double time. He felt his fingers shaking and watched as drops of red stained his shorts.

Did I get shot? No, I must have been cut from bits of glass when the window shattered.

Curtis watched as the van's interior and road beyond roll high to the right and again to the left as if he was at the helm of a fishing trawler out off George's Bank in the northern Atlantic.

"Are you okay buddy? You don't look good," Zack said as he snapped closed his cell phone. "You're bleeding."

Curtis tried to assure Zack he was okay, that it was just a little cut from flying glass, but instead he only mumbled something unintelligible. Then, finally, the world rolled heavy to the right and went black.

Curtis awoke a few minutes later with hot, dry air flooding the van and a man wearing a blue and white paramedic's uniform standing in his opened door pressing a white strip of sterile gauze to his forehead. Still sitting in his seat, Curtis rolled his eyes around to get his bearings.

"Where are we?" Curtis asked.

"I pulled into a checkpoint; we were only two kilometers away," Zack said from somewhere outside.

The paramedic removed the gauze and replaced it with a square patch band-aid.

"You're lucky; that bullet just grazed your head," the paramedic said in a strong eastern accent. "It's not deep — it just bleeds a lot. Probably won't even need stitches."

The man then turned to Zack and directed him to take the Canadian to the hospital in Hebron for a closer check-up.

"Sure," Zack replied in Hebrew.

The remaining drive to Hebron was quiet. Curtis knew he had crossed the line earlier and he was hoping it didn't result in him having to find another ride back to Nevatim. As they approached the city, Curtis realized it was far larger than he was expecting. Off into the distance Curtis could see large marble and limestone quarries. Closer to the highway there were rows and rows of grape and fig trees.

As they turned left off Hwy 60 and onto Gur Ayre road in the old town of Hebron or *Kiryat Arba*, Zack asked him where he would like to be dropped off.

"Well, I don't know the area. So I will just go with you to your cousin's shop. Then it will be easy for me to find you when it's time to leave."

"Okay," Zack replied.

Inside Curtis exhaled. *Phew!*

The city of Hebron is home to over 160,000 people, and about 500 are Israeli settlers living in the Old Quarter. As they drove through the circular round-about, Curtis's head began to swim. He was getting a strong sense of déjà-vu. Perhaps the shock of almost being killed was setting in. His heart began to beat faster, so he took a few deep breaths until his head cleared.

Good.

They passed the Kiryat Arba Local Council building and around another round-about, on the corner of Sderot Kalev Ben Yefune Street, was the Hebron Kosher Meat-Poultry & Deli. Zack pulled the van up right in front of the store. Curtis noticed there were only a few people walking around the neighbourhood for such a large city: mostly armed IDF security. A young man in his mid-twenties came out to meet the van. He was tall and looked solidly built; as if he was a regular at the local gym. Wearing a Hawaiian shirt, army camouflaged cutoff shorts and a bloody apron he came out and gave Zack a kiss on both cheeks. It struck Curtis odd that he had hardly seen an adult over thirty years old since he arrived in Israel. Perhaps this far out from the major centers, only the young and adventurous dared to make a go at it. Whatever the reason, his new perception left him feeling unsettled. In Hebrew, Zack said hello and motioned to Curtis, mentioning Canada. The man laughed and stuck out his hand. In a strong eastern accent he introduced himself as Joshua Goldstein and the owner of the Deli.

"Would you like to come in for a bite to eat while you wait? Delicious smoked kosher beef from a ranch outside Be'er Sheva. You like very much."

Curtis returned the introduction. "Thank you, but I am going to go for a walk and look around."

Curtis noticed a tattoo on Joshua's forearm. It was a black fist within the Star of David, surrounded by a yellow square.

"Nice tat!" Curtis motioned to his arm. "I think I saw something like that painted on some doors and walls coming into town.

Joshua looked over at Zack. "It's an old Jewish symbol. It means never back down, stand your ground, fight for what is yours — that kinda thing."

"Oh, right on." Curtis felt like he was missing something, as if it was an inside joke. Nevertheless he really wasn't that interested. Curtis watched as Joshua's eyes examined his patched forehead.

"You're head? You have wound?"

Curtis instinctively tapped the bandage and winced.

"Sand flees!" Zack interjected with a sadistic smile.

Curtis looked over at Zack. "Sand flees?"

Before Zack could answer, Joshua looked over Curtis's shoulder at the van. Rage filled his eyes and he sprinted to the blown out window.

Zack blasted out something in Hebrew. Joshua's arms

swung wildly from the van to the ground, then to the sky and back to the van, cursing loudly.

Zack described, what Curtis assumed, was the events of earlier.

"You're lucky," Joshua said between gritted teeth trying to gain some composure. "Sometimes those fucking flees will take off your head."

Joshua watched as some of his patrons from inside the deli stepped outside to see what all the commotion was about.

Two of the young men looked Curtis up and down in a way that made Curtis feel a little unwelcomed.

Zack walked into the deli; at the door he turned around. "How about three hours?"

"Sounds perfect," Curtis returned. *Just get me out of here.*

Curtis walked further down the quiet street taking notice of the dead businesses and complete lack of pedestrian traffic. He passed the Talmud Tora Grade School and turning up Yehoshua Bin Nun Street, he began to see some people walking around. As he approached an alley way he could smell a wonderful medley of spices, meats and flavoured rice. Down the alley there were dozens of people talking and laughing in what appeared to be an outdoor market. Tin sheets were bolted to the outer walls of buildings giving some shade to the vendors. Shabby tables were full of fresh produce, spices, breads and cured meats. It was only a few streets from the deli, but this seemed like a whole different city. Curtis wasn't so sure he could bring himself to eat anything from in there, but the carnival like atmosphere lured him in.

He was getting a feeling that he might not be in a safe area from the odd look he received by the first vendor. Even with kids walking by wearing their *Transformer* backpacks, he never felt fully safe until he noticed the Israel Defense Force had a guarded outpost on every three or four rooftops.

Spying a vendor that had small rectangular prayer rugs displayed around his shack, he walked over.

"Assalamu alai kum," Curtis said, remembering the phrase from his briefing and hoping he said it correctly.

"Alai kum Assalamu!" the shopkeeper replied as he tilted his head.

"I am sorry; that's the extent of my Arabic."

"That is OK" the man said in English. "Most of us here speak good English. I am Hasalem. What brings you to Kiryat Arba?"

Curtis's fight-or-flight response began to ease. He could see kindness in the man's eyes.

"Just sightseeing, but the fantastic aroma brought me into the market."

The man heartily laughed aloud, "Yes and my wife across the road there makes the best Musakhan in the West Bank. And those poor souls," pointing up to the guards, "have to put up with it every day. A good punishment, yes?"

It was Curtis's turn to laugh. He was beginning to like this man.

"What can Hasalem do for you today?"

"I wasn't thinking of buying anything today, but your rugs caught my eye."

The vendor slipped right into business mode, rubbing his fingers along the three-foot rug sitting on top of a pile of layered rugs in front of him.

"This is very good, very excellent rug. Feel for yourself. Real silk; hand woven here in Hebron." He picked the rug up rolled it back and forth in between his hands. "Look how the sun hits the rug at different angles, the different shine you get — that's real silk, my friend. Where are you from? America?"

"No, Canada."

"Oh, Canada. Beautiful country. I have cousin, Ahmed, drives cab in Montreal; very cold in winter time. So my

Canadian friend, I give you great deal. You buy two rugs, I give you hookah free."

Curtis laughed again. He had no doubt that the rugs were genuine silk and probably made here in the city, but he didn't really want a rug and definitely not a hookah. "I don't think so."

The eastern businessmen were true entrepreneurs and they never let you walk away without a good fight.

"OK, you don't like hookah; me neither. Hookah made in China — crap. How 'bout you buy two carpets, I throw in extra carpet free no charge."

Hasalem could see the pause in Curtis's eyes. He wanted to quickly seal the deal.

"And I add free meal from my wife. You like very much."

Without a second's wait, Hasalem yelled something in Arabic to his wife. He winked at Curtis, "You will like very much."

Hasalem's wife was dressed in a black Jelbab: a long Muslim dress that covers the entire body but leaves the face and hands exposed. She walked over with some zesty chicken and rice wrapped in thin Arabic bread and aluminum foil. It smelled spicy and looked delicious. Feeling obligated to accept the offering, Curtis thanked her. Hasalem smiled wide, knowing he was going to sell something today.

"Eat," he motioned to Curtis's wrap. Pulling out a slender silver tea pot and two small cups he placed the set on a cleared section of table.

"Here, sit, drink some tea, apple raspberry, very good, you like. Tea very good for head; help cure cut under bandage."

Curtis instinctively touched his head again.

"Hey, if it works I'll come back and buy the whole case."

Hasalem pulled out a folding chair so Curtis could sit down and enjoy his meal; he watched as Curtis took his first bite.

The flavours danced across Curtis's tongue. He had eaten

in the Middle East before, and even at Muslim picnics in the parks back in Halifax, but this was different. The spices tasted more alive, more exuberant and fresher somehow. It was hot — it was really hot — but with a Hungarian background, Curtis was no stranger to spices. Hasalem was looking for more of a reaction out of Curtis as he bit into the Musakhan, but oh well! Back to business. He leaned closer.

"So you buy two rugs, very cheap, my Canadian price; you don't tell no one. I throw in free rug. Now you pick which rugs you like."

Not being too familiar with haggling, Curtis was finding it very difficult to work up the courage to say no. He finally gave in.

"How much for ONE rug?"

CHAPTER SIX

Curtis picked up a sightseeing map from a vendor and continued his travels through the city with his ancient sandstone figurine and new "praying" rug under his arm he approached the street corner across the road to the Cave of the Machpelah. The sensation of his heart racing and his head swimming was beginning again. Curtis knew guys who came back from Afghanistan with Post Traumatic Stress Disorder, or PTSD, who complained of similar sufferings, but here he was enjoying a beautiful walk during a bright and sunny day in an ancient and exotic city and he felt like shit.

Perhaps he picked up some foreign spore or bug that his body was trying to fight off. Maybe it was the twelve inoculations he had to take within thirty minutes before he left on the plane to come out here. A biological soup percolating in his bloodstream — great, now *there* was a reason to panic.

The shrine was a wondrous site to behold to say the least, even though it reminded Curtis more of a prison facility with its high stone walls and two minarets as guard towers more than it did a holy site.

The Cave of Machpelah or Haram el-Khalil (Muslim Shrine

of the Friend) preserves the Tomb of the Patriarchs which is believed to be the burial site for Abraham and his wife Sarah, Isaac and his wife Rebekah, and Jacob and his wife Leah. In the first century B.C., Herod the Great constructed a shrine over and around the caves. Thirteen centuries later, Crusaders added to its splendor. Muslims refer to the shrine which is built around the caves as the Ibrahimi Mosque and believe that the tomb also holds the body of Joseph, the son of Jacob. The building is divided into two parts: one side for Muslims and the other side for Jews. Security is strictly controlled by the Israel Defense Force.

The Tomb of the Patriarchs is the second holiest site in all of Judaism next to the Temple Mount in Jerusalem.

Curtis stared at the large edifice, sweat beading on his forehead and his mind spinning even faster now; he knew something wasn't right. He felt his stomach twist and his lunch wanting a second chance.

Maybe that bullet rattled more than he first thought.

Then, as he stood on the corner, vomit erupted from his mouth. At that moment the hundreds of pilgrims who frequent the holy site daily froze in their steps. In the corner of his vision he noticed that a bird leapt from a branch and remained motionless in the air without flapping or falling. Even his vomit, with its cornucopia of colour and textures was frozen too, set in a mid-air arc.

Curtis blinked and looked around. He felt like he had become trapped in a digital photo of the neighbourhood.

I must have had a stroke. I'm dead, and any moment I will see the Light.

The city around Curtis pixilated and dissolved, and as it changed a new city emerged around him.

Slowly, the figures moved and the sounds flooded his ears. The image in front of him was one of panic and mayhem. It was night time and buildings all around him were on fire.

Men with swords and shields were battling giants directly in front of him. These great giants looked like they could easily defeat their foe but were grossly outnumbered, like a swarm of ants taking apart a Tarantula spider. Curtis suddenly felt the urge to get into the battle and help these men fight off this scourge, these colossal monsters. With his heart racing and adrenaline pumping he tried to move but couldn't; he could only stand there. Suddenly an enormous figure was running towards him. It had one arm wrapped around a woman who was obviously terrified, while the other arm clutched a leather holder containing a dozen scrolls. The woman was screaming, "Haduj! Where is my son Haduj?" and was trying to run back into the large palace. Even to Curtis, running back looked like a bad idea. The giants stopped directly in front of Curtis. The giant man grabbed the woman firmly by the shoulders. Curtis could see the panic in her eyes and feel the desperation flowing from her.

"I spoke with Haduj; he will meet thou at the well outside of the city," the giant said.

"And what of Sheshai? Will he meet us there also?"

"Sheshai gave himself to save thou and Haduj. We must go now while there is a great commotion before ALL is lost."

Curtis realized that it wasn't the giants attacking the city, but the men attacking the giants. The couple began to run again, and fled right through Curtis. As they did he felt them — felt their energy. He could smell the oils and perfumes on the giant woman, and the strength and dominance from the giant man. For that brief moment he shared in their fear and desperation. When the connection was broken, he experienced a sense of loneliness; like remembering a hug from an old lost friend. He watched them take a few more steps, when a large holler came from the direction of the palace. The giants stopped and turned, as Curtis looked back he seen two men exiting the rear of the palace. Together they held up the large severed head of a giant, his eyes rolled back into his skull and his mouth twisted in grief.

The woman began to scream in heart break and misery. "Sheshai! Sheshai! Ahiman, they killed Sheshai!"

Her cries hung in the air as the ancient world once again froze and the modern one materialized. Before Curtis could see it, he heard his vomit splash against the sidewalk. People walking by gasped in disgust. His head and stomach quickly settled but he stood there stunned, unable to rationalize what had just happened.

An entire battle took place directly in front of him. And those giants — he couldn't shake the feeling that he somehow knew them, which was absurd and impossible. And that huge dismembered head! Thinking of those eyes made Curtis's stomach lurch.

He had never seen that city before or anything like it, so ancient and yet comfortably familiar. He didn't know how he knew, but he knew that the burning city in his vision was the same city laid out in front of him now. The ancient palace may not be the exact same building as the Cave of Machpelah, but they shared the same plot of land.

Curtis didn't feel like himself. He felt different — that *hallucination* had an impact on him; it changed him somehow, and he decided to head back to the deli and hopefully back to the Israeli airbase.

CHAPTER SEVEN

Saskatoon, Saskatchewan

Feeling the back of his neck burning, Lukács Vadász squeezed sunscreen from a bottle and rubbed it on the sensitive area. Lying on the roof for two hours with no breeze in the Saskatchewan sun was hot but with his Camel Pack full of water and an inflatable mat, he was comfortable Plus, he had paid a bigger price to prove his devotion to duty. Last winter Lukács lost two toes to frostbite after he had hiked six kilometers on a Utah ranch to achieve his mission. This assignment was simple, but necessary. Peering over the edge of the Delta Bessborough Hotel with his Steiner 7x50 Commander XP binoculars, he scanned the park. There she was, right on time.

Every day right after school Stephanie La Pierre cuts through the public park along the South Saskatchewan River to get to her part-time job at Kelsey's Restaurant. Today she was alone and visibly upset. Yesterday she had a fight with her boyfriend, Mike, after she had confided in him about some very strange visions she was having. She thought since he had promised her that he would ask her to marry him, he would have been more compassionate with the changes she was going through. He thought she finally went crazy, like her old man, and dumped her on the spot. Already this morning Mike was holding hands with Sarah McNiven, her 'ex' best friend. Because her *waterproof* make-up wasn't quite up for the task, fixing it had her running late and she had to hurry.

Lukács put the binoculars down and picked up the L96 sniper rifle with its 3-12x50 sight and spotting scope and screwed on the silencer. The L96 is the new weapon of choice used by British military snipers in all of the British services. It fires a 7.62mm round with an effective kill range of 900m.

Taking off his glove, he rolled up his left sleeve. The hot June sun gleamed along the edges of his scar on the underside of his arm. The skin was shiny and smooth after the blistering healed. He ran his finger over the rampant lion and up to the two stars, and then along the seam of the crest. This has become a ritual before carrying out each task over the past ten years since he had been officially ordained into the KRÁJCÁR *Testvériség*. The divine goal to rid the world of demons and their human concubines is both benevolent and sanctioned by God and His dominion of angels. During his Swearing of Allegiance, or the '*Káromkodás Engedelmesség*,' to the ancient fraternity, the sacred branding implement shaped into the KRÁJCÁR crest is used to identify their elite priests. Not just anyone can join the Holy *Testvériség*. First, you have to be born into it. Then you have to be invited by one of the seven Lieutenants. And, finally, after you have "proved" your mettle — spiritually, by putting the Testvériség ahead of wealth, self and flesh and physically, by enduring extreme combat and military training and even torture. When and if you accomplish that, then you are "marked" with the coat of arms, a manner of baptism by fire and pain that both cleanses and renews your soul. If you fail to *prove* yourself then you have failed God and dishonoured the corps. Those who have failed have never been seen alive again. The secrets and mysteries that make up the sanctified KRÁJCÁR are far too righteous for the unworthy.

Pulling his sleeve back down and replacing his glove, Lukács cracked open the folding stock of the weapon. Placing his right eye to the scope and comfortably resting his cheek on the support, he found Stephanie approaching the tree line. He finely adjusted the sights to the back of Stephanie's head while whispering the KRÁJCÁR prayer, "Words of Strength.": "You are an abomination and the divine knowledge isn't meant for you. Now fuck off."

Lukács pulled the trigger on the L96. The silencer can hardly be heard from four feet away, let alone from the rooftop of the hotel. The precision bolt glided smoothly like it had dozens of times in the past and connected with the butt of the chambered round. Within a fraction of a second after leaving the muzzle, Stephanie La Pierre fell forward with a fine red mist still floating in the air where she last stood.

Staring at her lifeless body through the scope, Lukács had one thought of regret: the kill effectiveness of the L96 was too efficient. Most of these abominations never felt death's blow. They get *out* too easily, and he will have to change that.

***

Back at the airbase, Curtis was walking up the hallway to his room as Sgt Gilvery was knocking at his door.

"What's up Sarge?" asked Curtis.

The sergeant looked at Curtis and his souvenirs.

"While you were out shopping we got a call from Ottawa telling us the exercise was over and to head back to Canada ASAP."

Curtis was confused. This took over a year to set up and out of the blue they were being asked to leave.

"Why, what happened?"

"I don't know the full details," the sergeant said. "But it

has something to do with the Israeli Navy and a fleet of aid ships. The Colonel didn't get into it but we are out of here as soon as the C-150 is ready — in about three hours."

"It looks like I will be home sooner than I thought," Curtis said to himself.

As he entered his room he looked around. He noticed he hadn't really unpacked so he had time for a cold shower and quick nap.

Halifax, Nova Scotia (two days later)

Curtis stepped out of the shower; his head began swimming as if he had just taken a couple shots of a strong drink. He took another step closer to the sink and his heartbeat quickened.

What's going on? Curtis wondered to himself, remembering his experience back in Hebron.

Too many people today are just dropping dead.

It made him a little nervous. There was a soft rumble outside in the distance.

"Curtis, are you out of the shower yet?" Vivica called from down stairs. Her voice grounded him back to the present.

"Yes. Why? Do you need it?"

"No. There is a storm coming. We better get the flashlights and candles out. You know how unsteady the Nova Scotia power is."

"Alright, just give me a couple of minutes."

Curtis could hear the first few drops of rain hit the window. He reached up and wiped the steam off the mirror with a hand towel. He examined the scar that was already healing on his forehead. He could also see in the reflection of the mirror what looked like an outline of a face in the bathroom window. Turning, he got a closer look to examine it. It looked as if someone literally pressed their face against the window pane. He could make out the outline of the jaw, cheeks, a nose and a smudge of a forehead. It didn't strike him as anything sinister or peculiar — Charlie probably drew it during her last bath. Curtis thought he would add a mustache to her self portrait and tease her about how cute she would look with one, but when he got up closer to it he noticed the outline was on the outside of the window.

"Vivi, look at this!" Curtis hollered, thinking she was still down stairs.

"Look at what?" she said standing right behind him. It scared Curtis enough so that he dropped his towel. Behind Vivica, Charlie shouted, "Daddy, I see your bum."

There is one thing you can always count on with children; they will always be around at the most inopportune time, Curtis thought.

Not really interested in bending over to grab his towel, Curtis side stepped himself in front of Vivica.

Vivica turned around to Charlie, "Get out of here you! Go back to your colouring."

Charlie turned and ran into her room laughing.

"Great! That'll give them something to talk about at daycare tomorrow," Curtis said finally reaching down for his towel.

"Look at what, exactly?" Vivica asked returning back to the original conversation. Curtis pointed to the outline on the window.

"What about it?"

"The face there, do you see it?" Curtis questioned.

"Of course," Vivica replied. "And a very nice likeness too."

Curtis looked back at her. "I didn't draw it. And it's on the outside." He reached up and tried to wipe the chin off with his hand.

"That's creepy!" Vivica exclaimed. "But that can't be a face. We're on the second floor. There isn't even anyplace to stand out there." Thunder boomed again outside and the rain picked up.

"I don't know. It's pretty weird," Curtis said. He reached over and drew in some eyes with the remaining steam on the windows.

"We better get those candles soon." Vivica no sooner said that when lightning flashed outside. The lightning lit up the whole backyard through the window, except for the face. It was as if the person was still standing there. Curtis could feel the hairs on the back of his neck straighten up. Vivica yelped and dropped her flashlight. The two of them stood there dumbfounded. The next flash lit up only the eyes that Curtis drew in earlier. Then the outline slowly washed away with the rain. Vivica slowly looked over at Curtis.

"I will go and get Charlie some cereal before bed."

Curtis was still looking at the window. "Okay, but you are waiting right here until I am done toweling off; you're not leaving me in here by myself."

The next day Curtis got a call from Eavery.

"Hey Curtis, what's up?"

"Hi Eavery, I got a few days off for all that hard work on the weekend. Too bad you never got much of story."

"So is the life of a journalist," Eavery returned. "Are you busy? I was thinking that maybe we could get a coffee down at Tim's on Portland Street? My treat."

It is a well known fact within the Canadian Forces that Tim's refers to Tim Horton's, and it is equally understood that you never turn down a *free* "Tim's."

Within the hour Curtis and Eavery were sitting together at the coffee shop. After a few minutes of pleasantries, Eavery pointed towards Curtis's scar. "You know, you never did tell me how you got that."

"This? Oh, sand fleas."

"Sand fleas?" Eavery thought for a moment. "Oh...you mean desert snipers. You're pretty lucky; I understand their bite can be deadly."

"Yeah, so I've heard."

"So how are you feeling over all? Feeling any different?"

Curtis took the plastic lid off the cup. "How do you mean?"

"Do you feel different? Have you seen things that maybe freaked you out? Are you sensing things that perhaps you never noticed before?"

Curtis looked across to Eavery Flashes of his vision back in Israel and the face on his bathroom window betrayed his composure.

"That's a bit vague," he stammered. "But... no, I don't think so. Why would you ask that?"

Eavery decided to cut through the crap and leaned over to Curtis. "Because you look different; your 'aura,' for the lack of a better word, has changed colour. That means *you* have changed. I have seen it before — many times, actually. Are you saying nothing interesting happened while you were in Israel?"

Curtis could feel his face start to turn red. He did not want to tell anyone what happened in Hebron, or after his shower. Actually, for the first time, he put the two incidents together. He began to feel even more unbalanced.

Eavery, sensing his discomfort and how unsettled Curtis probably was, decided to confess a little of his own experiences.

"Curtis, listen. I can tell that something happened over there. Let me guess — while over in Israel you had a very strong urge to go see Hebron?"

Curtis looked at Eavery with a sense of startled confusion. *Why would Eavery say that?*

"And when you drove into Hebron, you had feelings of nostalgia, which probably confused you since you never have been there before. Sound accurate?"

Curtis didn't say anything; he just looked at Eavery.

"And you had an extremely intense hallucination, maybe

near... an old temple or some obscure lonely tree. How am I doing so far?"

Curtis rapidly flashed back to his vision. It was impossible for anyone to know this ever happened to him. Eavery watched Curtis's stunned face and knew he was right.

"Something similar has happened to a lot of people throughout the centuries. It wasn't a hallucination; it was more of a 'remembering.'"

Eavery's last comment snapped Curtis out of his thoughts. "Remembering? I have never been to Israel before, or even seen anything like that in a documentary," Curtis barked, a little more aggressive than he meant too. He looked around the busy café and was feeling very uncomfortable with the direction this conversation was going and how Eavery could possibly know; he never even told Vivica. Looking around to see if anyone noticed his outburst he leaned closer over the table.

"How do you know what happened?"

Eavery rested fully back against his chair. "I told you. It's happened to a lot of people. And once that *remembering* occurs, your whole world is going to change."

"Like, how?"

Curtis began to feel like his mind was slipping, as if reality was so delicate it could be pulled out from under him, and that he might wake up one day a homeless schizophrenic living alone on the street. "Will I start talking to myself or hear voices when I am alone?" His stomach started to twist and feel nauseous.

"Yes, but you won't be alone. And you will have more intense *rememberings* — just out of the blue."

Curtis did not like how coy Eavery was acting, and he suppressed the urge to reach across the table and punch him in his smug mouth. Eavery watched Curtis's eyes. He looked scared and was becoming defensive.

"Alright, listen. I am going to tell you what's going on."

This time Eavery looked around the café. "First of all, take a deep breathe and relax, you are not going 'mental.' How familiar are you with the Old Testament?"

Curtis blinked. "What? The Old Testament? What the fuck are you talking about?"

"Okay!" Eavery put both hands up in defense. Standing up he looked down at his full cup of his coffee that Curtis actually ended up paying for. "Damn it's been a long time since I had a cup of coffee. Let's go for a walk and gets some air. I will tell you everything."

Curtis still felt as if his world was collapsing around him. He didn't want to go anywhere, and he didn't want to talk to Eavery about this anymore. He wanted to go home, kiss his wife and daughter with the last bit of his sane mind, hoping to save that memory when reality has been completely taken from him and he is left drooling in a straight jacket somewhere.

Eavery could see the distance in Curtis's face. "Listen, just down the road is an awesome pub: Celtic Corners. Let's go and have a few beers and I will fill you in on everything."

The thought of a few beers and maybe a few shots of rum sounded good. Curtis stood up and followed him out towards the door.

"You know if that scar on your forehead heals into a lightning bolt, you could make a lot money doing impersonations."

"You're fucking hilarious," Curtis said as he gave Eavery a shot in the shoulder.

CHAPTER EIGHT

Membertou, Cape Breton Island
7 years ago

John Christmas, or J.J. as his father calls him (because he was named after John Christmas senior, who was also named after his father and grandfather), or Jack Frost as his friend Jerry calls him, or John Constantine as he calls himself (because, like the comic book hero, he too can see demons and angels) is a sci-fi junky. He had every season of *Babylon 5*, all five seasons of *Stargate: Atlantis*, and both seasons of *Stargate: Universe* on DVD and in graphic novel form, plus two limited edition episodes of *SG: Atlantis* with alternate endings that couldn't even be purchased in North America (but he has a friend who has a friend who knew some guy who picked up an 'original' copy while travelling across Egypt), John/Jack/John didn't fit the stereotypical mold of a native kid from Membertou, Cape Breton.

At eighteen years old with over eleven thousand comic books he decided to open his own science fiction/fantasy/medieval war dungeon called VADER'S CAMELOT. Initially, it started out as a safe room from the outside world that couldn't appreciate his love for the genre and showed him by ridiculing and beating the shit out of him at every opportunity. It was a place where he could sit with his vast collection of books, posters and action heroes, allowing the creative energy from the master authors like Alan Moore and Winslow Mortimer melding his mind with the mind of Dr. Manhattan from *The Watchmen*, or stand side-by-side a freshly resurrected Arthur Pendragon, King of the Britons, while he battled the alien scourge in *Camelot 3000*.

Today, the book store is the largest graphic novel supplier on the island and the second largest east of Montreal. Last year, the Island Knights of Andromeda (a science fiction social group John created when he was twelve years old consisting of his three friends from school and three newbies from Whitney Pier and Port Hawkesbury — one of which was a white girl who was a very enthusiastic fan of *Xena: Princess Warrior* and a first girlfriend) took a road trip to the world's largest comic book convention: the Comic Con in San Diego, California. This year the IKOA already had tickets for the *Star Trek* convention in Las Vegas, Nevada, celebrating 45 years of the *Trek*.

The Membertou band is the largest and wealthiest of the Mi'kmaq tribe in Nova Scotia. With its upper class Trade and Convention Center, the Membertou Advanced Solutions and Membertou Market, the reserve is well established within the city of Sydney. John Christmas, the IKOA and Vader's Camelot has also benefitted from the symbiotic relationship of cultures.

The Mi'kmaq, and more specifically the Membertou band, has had a long history as "watchers." When Cape Breton Island was colonized by the Europeans, an intense imbalance corrupted the natural flow of the divine breath. The *Muin*, the *Tiam* and the *Kitpu* spirit guides who had once easily connected with their earthly brethren were being forgotten and turned into legends and myths. As a last resort, John's great grandmother was indoctrinated as a kind of ambassador and exorcist by the Great Spirit, Kji Niskam. As a result, her supernatural gifts were carried down through her family and into John.

The ancient stories of John's family only isolated him more from the rest of his modernized band; he was a minority inside a minority. Therefore, John Christmas learned very early to keep any visions he had to himself and off of the play ground. Still, rumours flowed through the Christian school which, at the time, was run by Catholic priests and nuns — rumours that fueled Church's desire to convert his pagan heart and spread the salvation of Jesus Christ throughout the reserve.

It was this kind of isolation that drew John into the arms of Princess Leia, Luke Skywalker and Han Solo. While most of the other boys in his neighbourhood were out stealing their old man's whiskey and getting drunk in the woods behind the school, John was at the helm of the Millennium Falcon, as the first Native in space. As he watched Denis, J.C., Peter-Paul and a half dozen other boys in his class become teenage fathers, he was building his comic book collection.

The nights when John's father would return home after a two week binge from God knows where, smelling of home-made whiskey and stale cigarettes, trying to force himself on John's mother (who could handle her own until the yells and screams turned into slaps and punches), John Jr. would hide in a safe room he created in his closet between the far wall and two stacked milk crates with a thin, not-so-new comforter pulled over his head, like a hunter on the edge of a marsh secure behind a duck blind.

There, John would free himself reading the classic space adventures of Buck Rogers in the twenty-fifth century, the 1933 version, not the newer 1995 rewrite. He would also transport himself out of the two bedroom bungalow with no front storm door (three years earlier a hurricane travelling up the eastern seaboard skipped around Halifax and landed voraciously on Cape Breton), to a Bajoran space station called *Deep Space 9* run by Commander Benjamin Sisko.

Then, one fateful night in 2001, less than three weeks before John's sixteenth birthday, the chunky and uncoordinated John Christmas IV was awakened in the middle of the night by a large crash. John felt the whole house shake even deep in his sleep. Seconds later, he heard his mother yelling and cursing. John sprang out of bed and into the living room where his mother stood screaming hysterically at the destruction in front of both of them. John Christmas senior had driven their 1989 Buick Skylark into their kitchen, punching a hole into the west wall, wiping out the counter and upper cupboards, and destroying her table with its two mismatched chairs and one original chair (not that it mattered anymore). The car collided with the baker's rack and sent the microwave flying through the glass patio doors.

Above all, John Christmas Senior had destroyed what appeared to be all twenty-five of Terry Christmas's authentic Elvis Presley decorative plates, which she shrined on that very wall — twenty-five plates that represented twenty years of Christmases, birthdays and anniversaries. Five years of saving up enough money to vacation three days down in Memphis, Tennessee at the *King's* very own Graceland, and bring back a Royal Dalton exclusive "Jail House Rock" platter, tea cup and saucer set. Twenty-five plates that meant to her twice — no, thrice — what her marriage did. And that asshole drunk just destroyed the only thing (besides her precious John Jr., of course) that brought joy in her life.

The car had entered deep into the kitchen, well past the front doors and even some of the back doors. The steam from the radiator billowed out from under the crumpled hood and crushed grill, rolling and tumbling in front of the one still-working headlight and the only source of light within that half of the house. The Buick Skylark sputtered and coughed as it tried to survive the traumatic impact. The car eventually became silent, its damages far exceeding its ability to maintain itself. It sat there hemorrhaging its coolant onto the kitchen floor among the broken legs of the table and chairs, chunks of gyprock and insulation, and the shards of twenty years' of Elvis Presley decorative plates.

John Sr. lifted his head from the contorted steering wheel. Blood trickling from a gash on his forehead, but was rapidly flooding his face. John Jr. stood beside his mother, frozen at the spectacle in front of him. Terry ran over and flicked up the kitchen light switch. A four-bulb chandelier hung above where the table once sat, miraculously unscathed. They both watched as John Sr. pushed and shoved open his door and exited the wreck. Oblivious to the mass destruction that he caused around him, or even the blood pouring out of his head, he clumsily reached back into the car and pulled out his Browning .308 hunting rifle from the front bench. Standing and swaying for a moment, he took a step to the side and fell face first into a pile of rubble on the kitchen floor. Trying to stand once again, he began laughing at himself as he used his rifle as a support crutch. Not sure what to do first, Terry grabbed the phone and dialed 911. John Jr. ran over to his father, climbed over the broken counter and scattered pots and pans.

"Here, let me help you," he said as he put his arm under his father. John Sr., still laughing and unaware of his surroundings, began telling his son, J.J., all about the ten point buck in the trunk of the car and the good eats they were going to have as soon as his lazy mother gets the fuck back from bingo.

Now, with the house quiet but still filling with the pungent odour of steaming antifreeze, Terry put the phone down and continued with her yelling. With adrenaline rushing through his system and pumping through his ears, John Jr. could feel his mother's rage but only make out a few words: ...drunken asshole...fucking looser...that's it....out of here.

John tried to maneuver his father around the debris of the kitchen which now resembled a bombed bunker. Straightening a chair, John sat his father down.

"Woman! Oh there you are. I've got a buck in the trunk. Fry up the kidneys for me and J.J.," he slurred, still completely unaware of the devastation and her screaming.

Terry Christmas turned away, her heart and head pounded and her throat was coarse and sore. Deep down inside of her, the final connection of love and loyalty to the man bleeding in *his* shattered kitchen snapped. The final ghost of a promise made long ago during better times had been exorcized, and in its place a sad and sorrowful hole. Not a hole of loneliness and self-pity, but a cavity — no, an ulcer, created from the regret of an exhausting and bitter life: a life of being the wife of a severe alcoholic. As she left the kitchen and approached the front door, she had already decided to leave. She would stay at her sister's and not return — not for her clothes, not for her jewelry, and not even to check if any Elvis Presley decorative plates survived the crash.

There was an overwhelming feeling of freedom to finally leave. It was a decision she made years ago, a decision she made countless times only to retract it, like a promise made by a politician and discarded the day after winning the election. The 'snap' of the tether that leashed her to her *ex*-husband also liberated her conscience from her body. She floated above herself, watching in slow motion as her avatar left the wreckage of both the kitchen and her marriage to the door full of promise and sovereignty. Like a prisoner finishing her last seconds of her sentence, she approached the front gate a free woman. It was a fifteen-year incarceration, but she was guilty of committing only one crime: sticking it out.

With each foot fall closer to freedom flashed a regretful and troubled scene that had been stored in her brain like a video library of the last fifteen years. Each playback solidified her decision to leave.

John Jr. heard the *snap* too. It felt like the ultra-subsonic pop of a sprinter's tendon, followed by the release of all that built-up tension. He watched his mother's face and posture change from being tense with rage and disgust to calm and unconcerned. But the relief that *snap* had surely created in his mother only created loneliness and uncertainty for him. As John watched his mother turn and leave, he knew she had finally had enough; she was not coming back. He would be left here with a father he barely knew and respected less. He couldn't let her walk out the front door without promising to come back for him. He will stay tonight and look after John Sr., watch to make sure he doesn't drown in his own vomit or pass out with a lit cigarette in his hand and burn the house down. As his son, he was still held by a very thin hair of commitment. But even at fifteen, John wanted to be with his mother; he still needed to be with her. When she left the kitchen, John needed to tell her, "come back for me tomorrow; don't leave me here in *my* prison cell."

John Sr.'s head swam. He vaguely understood he was sitting on a chair, maybe in his kitchen, or maybe at a campfire. There is a lot of smoke. He smiled heartily as he wobbled in his chair, trying to support himself with his rifle in his right hand and waving at the steam with his left. Fragments of the last eight hours floated past his thoughts in a cloudy and random sequence. He did remember that he shot a buck and that he was hungry and that the bitch was supposed to fry him up some kidneys.

She was here just a minute ago.

"Woman, where the fuck are you?" he slurred incoherently.

In a completely involuntary muscle collapse, John Sr.'s head jerked back. While staring at the floating chandelier, he tried to reposition himself on the chair and drastically over-compensated, flinging himself forward into the broken table and ceramic plates. Still holding tight to his rifle, small pains in his hands and knees made their way through the fog of his brain. For the first time he became slightly aware of the slick wetness running down his face.

John Jr. got as far as the kitchen door when he heard the crash of his father fall onto the floor. Watching as blood streamed down his father's face and broken debris stuck in his hand, John Jr. was at a crossroads.

To his left was his mother, zombie-like and walking out the front door. To his right was a demolished kitchen, 2/3rds of a car and his bleeding, pitiful father.

On one hand, John stays and cleans up the mess that is his father and his home. He becomes the parent. On the other hand; John leaves with his mother and stays the young-minded teenager. At that moment John realized that his decision — and it *was* entirely his decision — was going to alter his life. In two seconds, the John of the present (the fifteen year old John with two parents) will cease being, and a new John will take his place. The extent of his change he didn't know — couldn't know. He could never have foreseen what happened next.

John Sr. sat on the floor in his kitchen, blood and alcohol blurred his vision. He rubbed his left hand on his lap trying to brush off the annoying stings and prickles of the embedded fragments of broken glass and wood. The image of his son, J.J. floated pass his vision like a blending of two channels on a black and white T.V. set, and J.J. reminded his brain of the buck he had shot earlier in the day (or was it yesterday?) With that memory surged the pride of the kill.

"Raaaahh!" he gave a warrior's roar. "Kji Niskam-Great Spirit was with me today, son," he mumbled out loud. "Kji Niskam filled my lungs with His breath." John Sr. inhaled deeply. "He took my arm and steadied my hand." He played the scene with his rifle reliving the earlier hunt. "And with the great mercy that only the Kji Niskam can give, he offered up his sacrifice." As if being time warped into the past, John Sr. was back crouching in the forest. Ahead of him was the ten point buck. Saying a prayer to the Great Spirit and thanking Him for His offering, John Sr. skillfully pulled the trigger. The crack of the .308 rang loud in his ears and in the kitchen.

John Jr. stood in the doorway undecided in which direction his life should go: a decision that was made for him. When the 7.8 mm slug from the Browning BAR Mark II Light Weight Stacker .308 Caliber short action rifle struck him in the chest. The John Jr. of the past was gone.

The intense blast of the rifle being discharged inside the house snapped Terry Christmas out of her daze like a pin popping a balloon. With the freedom of the door inches away, and a new life on the other side of it, she quickly turned around and watched as her son, the only pride left in her life, was launched from the doorway and sent into the hall. The self-preservation that consumed her only moments ago turned into guilt for almost leaving her baby, and then to panic for losing him.

Terry quickly ran to the hallway and collapsed next to her crumpled child. Pulling him face up and cuddling him onto her lap, she screamed as she applied pressure on the open chest wound billowing red blood.

John Jr. coughed and choked on his own blood as he stared at his mother's panicked face. His ears didn't register the bang from the rifle and his brain hadn't yet told his spirit that his body lay dying on the floor. So confused about what had just happened, he was still unaware that he was no longer standing in the doorway.

Completely unconcerned for her own safety (perhaps from another shot from that murderous bastard), she held her baby in her arms and screamed the name of Kokokwes, her spirit guide, to save her son. She cried to the Great Spirit that this was wrong, that John Jr. was too young, and that this rips a fucking hole in the balance of all Nature.

On the floor in the dark hallway, with the pungent smell of steaming anti-freeze mixed with the fragrance of burnt gun powder, John Christmas Junior lay bleeding to death. His coughing and convulsions slowed as his muscles gave up and his breathing ceased to a slow exhale.

John's world went white. His pupils relaxed and fully dilated, the picture of his mother's face, contorted in agony and grief, faded away in a sanitary bleaching of his vision. He didn't notice the paramedics shoving an air tube down his throat to pump much-needed oxygen into his lungs, or their absurd pressure on the large entrance wound in his chest and even larger exit wound in his back. He didn't notice the RCMP storming the house, guns drawn at the ready, because someone else called in "shots fired."

He didn't hear them shout, "he's got a gun" and open fire in an unwarranted sense of self-defense (John Sr. was of no threat as he had already passed out, propped up against his chair with his .308 rifle resting on top of the broken table. He didn't hear them because John Christmas Junior the Fourth had died.

***

Sitting in a booth at the far side of the pub, the waitress dropped down two pints of ale. Curtis grabbed the glass and downed half of it. Eavery stared at his beer as if drinking it up with his eyes. Curtis watched the journalist ogle the foam capping the top of his glass. To Curtis, it looked as if Eavery was afraid of it.

"Listen, man, if you are on the wagon, don't tempt yourself. I have lots of friends who are alcoholics — the military is full of them." Curtis reached over with a mocking attempt to grab the glass. "It's not a big deal — I will drink it for you," he added tongue in cheek.

A large *crack* went off in the pub as if some kid lit a cherry-bomb. Everyone in the pub jumped at the bang. An elder lady in a pink and purple flowered pastel suit sitting with her husband grabbed her chest and gave a startled hoot, "Ooh, what was that, Dan?" The elderly man lifted his head and looked across to his wife. "Eh? Did you say something Mable?"

Eavery just continued to stare into the glass of ale, seemingly completely unaware of the noise. "Man! It's been a long time since I drank one of these." He reached down and wrapped his fingers around the pint glass as if feeling its cold and damp surface for the first time in his life.

Curtis shook his head still trying to clear it from the loud thunderous blast. He felt uncomfortably voyeuristic as he watched Eavery bring the pint to his lips and slowly sip the ale.

"Are you going to be okay with that? Perhaps the two of you would like to get a room...and be alone together?"

Eavery didn't even hear Curtis's comment; he was fully absorbed in the moment. With that one sip Eavery too drank down half the pint, and then he placed the glass down on its coaster gingerly; protecting the beer's delicate structure.

"Okay, bare with me here," Eavery said returning to Curtis as if none of that even happened. "Have you ever heard of the Nephilim? In the Old Testament? Daniel? Numbers?"

Curtis put down his beer. "Yes, of course I've heard of the Old Testament; my parents are Catholic. Genesis and the beginning of creation, God's words and all that stuff, sure, but the Nephilim...no."

Eavery continued, "Well, around 2500 B.C. angels from heaven had sex with human females. Their offspring were massive giants. They created great cities throughout what

81

is today Israel, Jordan and Lebanon, and flourished for a thousand years."

Curtis was beginning to get impatient. "Heaven, angels and super human hybrids? Listen, Dan Brown, I don't have time for this."

"Curtis, this isn't a myth. These giants were real; their cities were real. They had trade routes throughout the Mediterranean. They farmed, mined and created a very comfortable life for themselves. Kiriath Arba was one of the main centers. The point is — they existed. The Old Testament, or what the Jews call the Torah holds the only known documents to describe them in any real detail. Around 1300 B.C., Moses ordered Jacob and Caleb to take over these cities. And they did, killing everyone they met. But some — a few — got away."

Curtis finished his beer and ordered another one. He wasn't in the mood to be listening to fairy tales but he was in the mood for the beer. Humouring Eavery, he asked, "Where did they go? And what does all this shit got to do with my hallucinations?"

Curtis felt the beer begin to make his head a little light. "Listen, I don't believe in the Bible. Old stories written by people who didn't know anything about weather, ocean currents, stars or galaxies so they made shit up like fairies, magical amulets, and pet gods to do their bidding."

Eavery began to sense this was going to be a harder sell than he expected. "Yes, Curtis, those people may not have had the same knowledge about science and nature as people do today, but they didn't have a child's mentality and they weren't stupid. The Nephilim that escaped carried within them divine DNA — their angelic heritage, so to speak. History is full of them; they stand out. Goliath, as in David and Goliath was a descendant. They are around even today — people who seem to be too big to be real, like that Chinese basketball player dude."

The waitress came by again, Eavery ordered some of their famous Brenton ribs (a delicacy he very rarely indulges in — but today was going to be an exception), and Curtis ordered another beer and some chicken wings.

"So what — we just look for really tall people and tell them that they have angel blood, and hope not to get our asses kicked. You know this long circle that you are taking me — telling me a whole lotta shit that I don't care about — it's really frustrating. Get to the point, what does this have to do with me and how you knew about my hallucinations."

"You're *remembering* because you are descended from them, too."

"Oh really? The last time I checked I was 5'10" — not really a 'tower' of a man."

"The blood line has been deluded for thirty-three hundred years or more. You are far more human than angel, but that little bit that remains in you has been awakened."

Curtis halted his sarcasm. As absurd as this sounded, he felt that Eavery was telling the truth.

Eavery continued, "You may have gone your whole life without ever *remembering* — I believe most people do, but you went back to your ancestral lands and that struck a note somewhere in your DNA and now you are becoming aware."

"Eavery, do you have any idea how ridiculous this sounds?" Curtis began withdrawing himself from the conversation. "So, what now? Do I develop some cool powers? Can we fly? Do we have superhuman strength?"

Eavery didn't like the tone Curtis was using, but he could understand why. Curtis was trying to cope with a whole new reality. Over the years Eavery watched many others go through the same adjustment.

"No Curtis, don't be stupid."

"Then what good is it? Why are you telling me all this?"

"Curtis, you have awakened a side of you that you never

knew existed. Some weird shit is going to start happening to you and I am trying to prepare you for it."

The waitress brought them their meals and for a few bites neither of them said a word. A two-man Celtic band started to set up their instruments on a small stage near the entrance.

Curtis put down his chicken wing and took a large drink of his ale. "So what kind of weird shit are you talking about?"

Eavery put his ribs down. "Well, more *rememberings* for one. Right out of the blue. You could be paying for a loaf of bread in a long line-up at the grocery store and all of a sudden you are standing beside a creek watching some giants water their huge grapes."

"Then what?"

"Then you're back at the cash register, people looking at you as if you're on drugs or maybe should be taking some. It can be very embarrassing," Eavery said.

Curtis was looking at him in disbelief. "Right out of the blue? No warning? What about if you're driving to work or somewhere? You could kill someone or yourself."

"Yes, you can. That happened to my good friend Frank; he rolled his car on the 103 near Timberlea. I suggest don't drive until you can control them better."

Curtis felt a little glimmer of hope. "Control them? We can stop them or something?"

The background noise inside the pub began to increase as more people started to funnel in and the band tested their equipment.

"No, you can't stop them. But you can kinda dilute the intensity a little bit, make them a little less... HD. Some can see through the visions and see what's going on around them here. Like a TV playing two movies at once, you can pay a little attention to both, but it's very confusing and very difficult to focus on just one.

Curtis took a deep breath, thinking back to his *remembering* and how it fully consumed him, how he was lost within it and how *it* let him go. Now finally giving his full trust over to Eavery, his thoughts were going over what he had said earlier.

"You mentioned my 'aura' changed, what do you mean by that?"

Finally, Eavery thought, *I broke through.* "I am about to go 'New Age meets physics' on you here, but don't withdraw on me. It is a proven fact that all living things — fish, dogs, humans — emit energy waves that can actually be measured. Psychics call it our aura."

"I understand energy waves," Curtis interrupted. "I deal with transmitted energy in the form of radio and RADAR waves on a daily basis."

"Exactly, then you can understand how different frequencies have different characteristics, faster or higher frequencies appear brighter and slower or lower frequencies appear darker."

"Yes, I can see that." Curtis found himself nodding.

"Precisely, some people *can* see it, and so will you." Eavery could see the wheels turning in Curtis's head.

"Why will I?"

"Because it seems to be one of the common 'gifts' that are shared. You must have noticed you went through some physical distress before your first *remembering* — puking and headaches, that kinda stuff? The synapses in your brain have literally changed; you can actually see the difference with a C.A.T. scan."

Curtis swallowed his last sip of ale. "And this change allows me to see people's auras?"

"Among other things…" Eavery's voice trailed off.

The waitress came by and removed the bone-riddled plates. "Is there anything else I can get you?"

The waitress' interruption snapped Eavery from his thoughts. "No thanks; just the bill."

The waitress looked over too Curtis.

"Just the bill is fine. Thank you."

Curtis was eager to learn more but the band testing their microphones broke his focus. He checked his watch and realized he had been gone for almost three hours.

"I gotta get back, and it's going to take me two hours to walk home. Vivi is gonna be pissed I left the car out this far."

"Yeah, I'm taking the ferry back to the Halifax side. Listen there is a couple of other people I want you to meet."

Curtis stood up and put some money down on the table. "Do you guys have some sort of club with secret handshakes and all that shit?"

Eavery shook his head. "No, it's not a club — just a group of people who share a similar history. They can help fill in a lot of the blanks. I will inform them and see about making some plans. Plus, I have a feeling you are going to have a lot of questions to ask."

"Me too."

"What's your cell number? I'll give you a call when I get the time and place."

"I don't have one," Curtis said nonchalantly.

"You... don't have a cell phone?" Eavery questioned with confusion thick in his voice.

"Nope, don't see any real use for it," Curtis said. He had seen that same expression on dozens of faces when others have asked the same question. It seemed to him that the world has gone crazy with cell phones. You put a phone in someone's hand and they either forget the basic rules for driving — keep your mind on the *road* — or the fundamental rules of etiquette — don't talk with your mouth full — and usually both.

The cell phone has become the new 'boob-tube', he thought. But the one thing that had Curtis shaking his head the most was 'texting'. Sure, it may be cheaper, but the very idea of *typing* someone a message when it was easier and more personal to actually talk to them seemed to contradict the reason for having a phone in the first place, and that was to *talk* to them.

"But aren't you a communications technician?" Eavery asked, still not sure if Curtis was putting him on or not.

Curtis waved his hand at Eavery. "Listen, you have my home number and I am sure you can reach me at work easily enough. Just let me know what's happening, okay?" He slipped out the door as the band just started into "Whiskey in the Jar"

"By the way," Eavery yelled, "they weren't *pet gods.*" But it was too late; Curtis had already walked out of the door.

Pet gods! That is ridiculous!

By the time Curtis got home Vivica had already started supper. Charlie was sitting on the floor playing with the sandstone figurine he brought back from Israel.

"Whoa! Charlie please don't play with that; it is very old." Curtis bent over and took the ancient doll.

Charlie started to pout. "But I like it. It's very warm and it makes me happy. And Barbie was going to marry him."

Vivica popped out of the kitchen and gave Curtis a kiss. "I didn't hear the car pull in… are you drunk?"

"I wouldn't say drunk, per se, but I drank too much to drive. We'll have to take a cab later to get it."

Returning back to the kitchen to stir her spaghetti sauce, Vivica said "I won't get pissy because it would have been worse if you had have driven. Were you with your new friend Eavery?"

"Yes! We ended up getting a bite to eat at the Celtic Corners. Sorry."

Vivica poked her head around the corner, "So when do I get to meet this new friend of yours? He is a man right? You haven't been running around with some strange woman?"

"Yes, he is a man, darling," Curtis replied in a *there is nothing to worry about* tone.

He is probably a man.

"Maybe I'll have him over for a BBQ."

"Don't forget I am heading off to Ireland again next week, hopefully to finish our mineral study of the Giants Causeway."

"Vivi, I forgot all about it. With Israel and... everything — it totally slipped my mind."

Vivica walked over and gave him a kiss. "I thought as much. I've got the baby sitter on standby if you need her."

Turning on the T.V., and switching it to the *Discovery Channel*, Curtis sat down with a tea. Charlie was playing with her Barbies at his feet. On the show, archeologists were talking about a new find on the island of Santorini, just off the coast of Crete in the Mediterranean.

Curtis was sitting in his chair completely enthralled with the documentary. As the camera man showed the perfectly preserved frescoes inside the Keftiu homes, the professor of ancient history who was narrating the documentary explained that they were not yet able to decipher the ancient text, but believed it to be an advanced Demotic script used by the Egyptians — possibly one of the missing links in humankind's language evolution. The script flashed across the screen. The inner voice in Curtis's mind read the script.

"Oh" Curtis said aloud, "the man Susemon was a fisherman, his wife was a beautician in a local spa, and their three children were students at the Earth and Space Institute."

"What's that dear?" Vivica asked from the kitchen.

"What Vivi?"

Vivica peered around the corner. "Were you talking to me?"

Holy shit! I just read that. I didn't just read it, I read it easily. And I read it aloud.

Curtis slowly pulled himself from his amazement. Looking over to Vivica, "Ah... no, I was talking to Charlie." He answered her with his voice flat and lacking interest as if he were miles away.

How could I have read that? I must have made that up. But I didn't make that up; it really said that Susemon was a fisherman, his wife was a beautician and his kids were students at the Earth and Space Institute. This has got to be part of the changes Eavery was talking about going through, reading ancient script. Okay, I need some air.

Curtis's head began to spin.

"Vivi, I am going to go for a walk, I'm not feeling good."

"Alright, but supper is almost ready." Vivica poked her body out of the kitchen swinging a wooden spoon, "And don't you dare give me a cold or something before I head to Ireland."

"I don't think it's a cold," Curtis said as he stepped outside. *Earth and Space Institute?*

CHAPTER NINE

Veszprém, Hungary

Gergõ Mátyás was sitting on a bench at the base of the old Fire Tower. This seventeenth century edifice was the second tallest structure in *Veszprém* next to the twin gothic peaks of the St. Michael's Cathedral. Every day at 2 p.m., Gergõ sips his cocktail of iced espresso and Royal Tokaji wine while listening to the enchanted melody composed by Antal Csermák, broadcasted from external speakers mounted on the tower. His thoughts drifted lazily in and out of ancient glory days: days when the Huns were seated at the center of Europe and Asia; days when Attila brought a million nomadic tribes together and forced Rome to its knees. Gergõ brought the glass back up to his lips and noticed some tourist mumbling to themselves and gawking at his deformed skull. A rage burned inside of him.

These fucking peasants have no idea who I am, where I am from and the power within my hands.

Under his breath he recited the Holy Szeklic prayer that Attila taught his youngest son, Ernakh, for strength and focus.

He reached into his suit pocket and retrieved a small,

pearl-handle pocket knife. Setting his cocktail aside on the bench, he swiveled the small blade erect and felt it *pop* as it locked into position. Grasping the pearl handle in his left hand, he placed the fine blade into his right palm. Seemingly disinterested with the tourists around him, he slowly and meticulously ran the blade from the webbing between his thumb and index finger down to the center. As the blade travelled down his hand he could feel the razor's edge divide the skin in a straight, surgical incision. At only a few millimeters deep, his hand didn't immediately surrender its crimson asset until he fanned open his fingers and thumb.

He watched as the pale skin around the wound turned red and then blood, in segregated droplets, finally breached the surface. With each pump of his heart, blood exited the slit, ran down the meaty part of his palm and dripped onto the ground.

After four or five seconds, Gergõ Mátyás pulled a silk handkerchief from his breast pocket and wrapped the wound. Satisfied, he disengaged the lock and closed the blade, re-pocketed the knife and continued sipping his drink.

"Jó reggelt kívánok *Vezető*!" Lukács said and he bowed his head as he approached his leader.

"Speak in English, Lukács; you need the practice. How did it go?"

"It vent… went… splendidly. All the istenverte…" Lukács paused to translate his thoughts. "…the *damned* have been sent back to hell."

As Lukács raised his head, he noticed a small pool of blood on the interlocked stone between the Vezető's feet and then the reddening handkerchief wrapped around his hand.

"Excellent!" Gergõ rubbed the length of his head with his left hand, wiping the perspiration that was forming.

"The virtuous Attila himself would be pleased of your accomplishments. I will need you to go back to North America."

"Vezető, you're hurt?" Lukács said his voice filled with concern.

Dismissing Lukács, the Vezető continued: "It seems that Almod has become careless and was captured by the American constabulary."

Lukács raised his head and looked up at the Vezető; he could feel the shame for his comrade flush his face. The strict canon law that all KRÁJCÁR brothers must follow is that when they are out exorcising the world and something goes wrong — like getting caught — they must take their own life to prevent any secrets from leaving the sanctified order.

"You wish me to eliminate Almod?" he asked disappointingly.

"No, my son, I have already taken care of that."

Lukács eyes returned to the Vezető's palm and again to the small puddle of blood at his feet. It is an ancient and honoured tradition carried on by the KRÁJCÁR, dating back to the funeral of Attila, that the Hun's cut their cheeks to honour Attila with drops of blood instead of tears.

"Our people in Montreal have informed me that Satan has been recruiting more lost souls to help him raise his kingdom on Earth. Almod's next assignment was in Halifax, Canada."

Halifax, Nova Scotia

As Curtis stepped off his porch and walked down the street, the fresh breeze off the Atlantic Ocean helped to clear his head. Around the corner was Fisherman's Cove, a small conglomerate of tourist shops, restaurants and fishing businesses. An acre or two of beach and sand grasses with a boardwalk made up a small conservation area where locals walk their dogs and the tourists take in the fresh air. On one side there is the view of the Atlantic Ocean, and on the other side in the distance is the city of Halifax.

Curtis sat down on a weathered wooden bench and surveyed the Halifax waterfront. The orange and white loading cranes at the pier, the iconic Purdy's Wharf, the Casino Nova Scotia, the naval frigates docked at the jetties, and the MacDonald Bridge stirred a little conflict within Curtis. This side of Halifax was quiet, slow and family oriented while that side of Halifax was bustling, energetic and full of dance clubs and excitement. Before Charlie was born, Curtis and Vivica lived on the Halifax side, enjoying all that the port city had to offer. When Vivica got pregnant, they decided to buy a home within the village of Eastern Passage. It saved Curtis thirty minutes in traffic to get to work; unfortunately, it added thirty minutes to Vivica's commute.

Looking at the twin blue and white towers along the wharf, Curtis noticed something he had never seen before: an incredibly large golden haze floated high above the city. With little industrial pollution — except maybe for the city's power plant — and an almost constant breeze coming off the water, the ominous cloud looked truly out of place.

What is that?

Curtis stood up and walked to the edge of the beach, tripping on thick beach grass and discarded clam shells. Unable to take his eyes off of the haze, he got lost in its complexity. It glittered above the city, as if golden metallic flakes were suspended high in the air. It had dimension and form in a continuously shifting structure, but as his mind accepted a form or building, the structures would lazily morph into something else, as if seeing a ghost drift through the fog. It extended up and along the coast line and looked every bit the size of the city itself. Curtis's brain was trying to understand what he was seeing, but there was no precedence of experience in which to relate it. It wasn't fog — of that much he was certain; it wasn't smog either. It looked like some ghastly apparition out of Stephen King's imagination.

That dreaded feeling of nausea and dizziness flooded Curtis again.

Oh no, now what?

Curtis could feel the hairs on his arms and back of his neck begin to stand. He slowly turned and watched as the chunks of tall grass and stones around him began to wave and distort as though he was looking through moving water. He could feel static build up in the air like he was standing at ground zero seconds before a lightning strike. And like a strike, Curtis was blinded by a wall of light and a blast of thunder engulfed him, disorienting his senses. When his eyes cleared from the flash, a massive figure stood directly in front of him. It was a truly perfect form, as if a black marble statue had come to life. Silver swirled within its skin, giving an impression of a constant churning just below the surface. An electrical field was discharging fingers of static along the ground around it.

Curtis looked up at the angel. He had a small linen-like cloth wrapped around his waist that covered down to mid-thigh, with tiny and almost translucent foreign symbols embroidered in gold within it. A thin leather belt strapped over his right shoulder supported a large leather satchel resting off his left hip. Curtis was in awe at the being standing before him and he couldn't prevent his jaw from dropping. Deep in his soul he could sense this creature held awesome power, but he also knew that the angel would not harm him. Feeling confused and awkward, Curtis clumsily mumbled, "hello."

The angel looked down at Curtis, "I am Jophiel."

As the angel spoke, Curtis was overwhelmed with emotions and he could feel tears rolling down his cheeks.

Curtis looked the angel up and down, and as he did, Jophiel unfolded his wings and spread them wide in triumphant grandeur, easily extending out fifteen feet. Curtis was astonished by its sheer size; he looked back into the face of the beautiful being.

"Curtis," boomed the angel, "you do not cower before me? You do not take a knee and bow your head with reverence at my sight? You are truly a son of Arba."

Curtis's head started to clear and his stomach settled. With his mind less fragmented he was able to see the overwhelming phenomenon that was now unfolding around him.

Curtis tried to speak but his throat was slower at recovering than the rest of him and only a squeak escaped his mouth.

"You — you are an *angel*!" It came out more of a question than a statement of the obvious. "You are standing here in front of me, you are so... huge!"

There was a sparking in Jophiel's eye and he reduced himself to a more appealing height of seven feet. "We sometimes forget how our size can affect humans."

Wow! Taking a deep breath Curtis looked around. There was an older couple walking their small dog along the farther half of the boardwalk.

"Did they see that?"

Jophiel turned his head and looked over. "No I am only appearing to you."

"Why? How? Why can't they see you and I can?"

"Because I *willed* it so. I have come to counsel only you."

Okay, Curtis thought to himself, *this must all be going on in my head. I am hallucinating again.*

"No," the angel replied to his thoughts. "I am standing before you and although these other humans cannot see me nor hear me, they certainly see and hear you."

"Did you just read my thoughts?"

"I do have that ability, but I have done this enough times that I could easily guess what you were thinking."

"Why have you come to me?" Curtis asked.

"Because you have changed; you are now looking through your eyes as the son of Arba."

95

"You mentioned that I was the son of Arba before. What does that mean?"

The angel took a step closer to Curtis. Even though he reduced his size, he was still a dominating seven feet and Curtis had to strain his neck to keep eye contact.

"Lets walk and I will explain it to you. Eavery has explained to you some of the mysteries that involve your heritage."

"Yes."

Removing a papyrus scroll from the leather satchel near his hip, the angel unrolled it and held it out for Curtis to read. At first the script was written in some prehistoric language, like something that might be seen on a Pharaoh's tomb in Egypt or on a clay tablet from ancient Mesopotamia. Then, slowly, as if Curtis was focusing a camera lens, he could read and understand the lettering.

"Arba was the first angelic human, meaning that his father was an angel and his mother was not. He was extremely powerful in both physical strength and intellect — at least by human standards. He created the House of Arba, and then his son Anak, and Anak's three sons Sheshai, Ahiman and Talmai begat the race *Anakims*. It was a vast empire that lasted for two thousand years. You have seen with your own eyes the destruction of the Palace of Arba and the slaughter of the innocent. When Ahiman, the grandson of Arba, escaped with his brother's wife and son they were able to save the angelic birth code that has made up the Nephilim race. Through time and breeding, the angelic code is now only a few genes diluted within a handful of scattered humans."

Curtis could hear Jophiel's voice trail off and he noticed a look in the angel's eyes that suggested he was remembering the past.

"A once great and advanced empire, over a million Nephilim lived amongst humans and thrived. Their trade network reached all corners of this world. Their knowledge of agriculture meant no one within the city walls ever wanted for food and their medicinal knowledge meant they cured many of the cancers that plague even your time."

Curtis could envision the utopia, and what it must have been like. Looking back at Jophiel, he watched the design in the angel's skin blend and roll; it mesmerized him, comforted him, like staring into a camp fire on a still night. Standing closer to him now, Curtis could see the being had no hair on his arms, legs or chest, and his skin was flawlessly smooth like polished glass.

What an incredible creature; it was easy to comprehend why earlier cultures would confuse them as gods.

"So why have you come to me, Jophiel?"

"I have already told you; you have changed. You have awakened your Nephilim side."

"But why does that bring *you* down to earth? Do you visit every person who has changed? Do other angels like Gabriel or Michael ever visit the Nephilim?"

Jophiel stopped and turned towards Curtis. "Yes, if they choose to. It so happens that *you* exist because *I* exist."

It took Curtis a few moments to understand what the angel just said.

Holy shit! He is my great, great grandfather.

Jophiel laughed aloud, this time he had actually read his thoughts. The thundering bellows forced the breath out of Curtis.

"It is a much greater distance between you and me then great, great grandfather. But you now understand what I am saying."

Curtis looked down, turning his hands back and forth, thinking he looked nothing like this magnificent immortal, he must take after his great, great grandmother.

"I heard angels fall in a certain hierarchy; where do I... uh, you fit... in to it?"

"There are three levels consisting of nine Orders. In the first level there are the Orders One, Two and Three; the second level has Orders Four, Five and Six; and third level is made up of the last three Orders."

"And where do you lie, if you don't mind me asking?"

"No of course I do not mind. I am in the Second Order, the Cherubim."

"The Cherubim?" Curtis asked, "Like in the Old Testament? Having the faces of a lion, an eagle, an ox and a man?"

"Yes, and the feet of a cow. I much more preferred the Assyrian description of a winged bull with a man's head. I personally never found anything wrong with a bull's head, but man must see himself in all that is great."

"So the Second Order, eh? Is that high?"

"We are second only to the Seraphim lead by Metatron."

Curtis realized he must have sounded like a child in the first grade with all his questions, but he couldn't stop himself.

"The Seraphim, they are powerful angels?"

"Their abilities are limitless, and Metatron's authority is second only to God. When Moses took his people out of Egypt, it was the Seraphim that held back the river, and it was Metatron who stood before the Egyptian soldiers as the pillar of fire, and again later as he inscribed in stone the laws given to the Israelites from Yahweh's own thoughts."

"Seraphim, Cherubim... What about regular *angels*?"

The old couple walked by, staring at Curtis; The old lady held their tiny dog tightly in her arms for its own protection.

Curtis guessed they had seen him walking around the boardwalk for the last several minutes talking to himself.

"I am rehearsing a play for... my daughter," Curtis stumbled out. Even he didn't buy it coming out of his own mouth.

There was a large smile spreading across Jophiel's face. "I never get tired of that."

Then he laughed aloud again. The old couple might not have heard him but their dog did, and Curtis swore that the dog was laughing at him too. The thundering laughter didn't affect Curtis as intensely this time as it did the last time; it was powerful but it wasn't overwhelming.

Through the angel's beautiful smile, Jophiel replied, "*Angels* are the last and Ninth Order; they are the most uncomplicated beings within the celestial realm and they are headed by Gabriel."

"I thought Gabriel was an Archangel?"

"Gabriel is a bit of an enigma; he fluctuates between Orders, which is why he leads the Angels. The Archangels are the Eighth Order, led by Michael."

Curtis could hear his name being called from a distance. He turned and he could see Vivica and Charlie standing near Main Street.

"Are you coming? Supper is getting cold."

Curtis had completely forgotten that Vivica was almost done supper when he left to get some fresh air. When he turned back Jophiel was gone.

Amazed by the disappearance, he glanced up to the stars; it was an uncharacteristically clear night. Then he jogged over to his family.

The next day at work, Curtis walked over to the kitchenette to refill his cup of coffee when he heard his name: "Corporal Papp?"

Curtis saw Sgt. Jerry Kraft walking towards him and he could see something very different about the sergeant today. He observed, more within his mind's eye than with his actual eyes, a colour variance about him: a faint pink hue engulfed the sergeant. The last time Curtis had seen Jerry was at the Israeli briefing. The sergeant was later replaced by another sergeant supply tech. And now Curtis was looking at Jerry in a very new way.

It was obvious that Jerry, too, was seeing Curtis in a different light. He knew that Curtis must have gone through the change from the difference in his appearance when Jerry saw him during the briefing to now, but he wasn't entirely prepared for Curtis's transformation. Curtis was engulfed in an aura, the same way as every one of them are, but Curtis's was significantly brighter. He radiated a bright yellow — an *almost* white.

Jerry had his change more than six years ago, back when he sailed in the Canadian Navy. HMCS Charlottetown had a two day stopover in Turkey. There he visited the ancient Roman city of Ephesus, and within the ruins he posed for a picture against some toppled stone pillars. It was there that Jerry's first *rememberings* took place. As it happens, like many things in life, coincidence and chance, past and present, and a little serendipity collided and a new fork in the road of destiny was created. That pillar and the majority of them within the ancient Roman Empire were created by a Nephilim master stonemason.

Within the last six years, Jerry has met several people whose Nephilim side had been awakened. But Curtis was different, that much he could see already. Most people's aura was pink or light blue — once he even saw a grey aura (not a good story) — but never had he ever met someone whose aura was bright yellow. A person's aura reflects his or her energy and the characteristics of a soul; the brighter and whiter the radiance is, the more intense and significant the power.

"Sergeant Kraft, right?" Curtis was a little surprised both by seeing the sergeant in the Headquarters building and seeing *his* orange aura.

"Yes, that's right."

"What brings you out to the Chiclet?"

"Oh, a little business with the pay office," the sergeant said still eyeing Curtis. "How was your trip to Israel?"

"Enlightening," Curtis replied, feeling uncomfortable talking about his experience, especially with someone he didn't really know.

"I can see that." Jerry took a step closer to the counter where Curtis was standing.

"We are having a get-together tonight with a few others who have been... *enlightened*. It's short notice but do you want to join us? We might have some answers to a few questions." Jerry let that last statement hang in the air.

"Yes, I sure do. Man, have I got to talk to somebody about what's going on! Where? When?"

Kraft was still eyeing Curtis a little suspiciously. "We try to get together at Lin's Wok once a week; it's a little Vietnamese restaurant down on Wyse Road near the bridge. Around six-thirty."

"Count me in," Curtis said.

"Good. See you then." Kraft turned and walked up the spiral stairs.

Curtis began to refill his coffee when he saw his friend Clyde Kiraly. Curtis exhaled heavily, pleased that Clyde looked like good ole' Clyde — no aura, no wings — just Clyde.

"Clyde!"

"Curtis, when did you get back?"

"Oh, a couple of days ago. Hey, when I was in Israel I picked up a small stone artifact for your son, Sean. Is he still into *old stuff*?"

"Yeah, he wants to study archeology when he graduates high school."

"Well, I have a feeling he'll love this. It's a few thousand years old, and it is probably illegal to have."

A mocking frown crossed Clyde's face. "Great, so you are trying to turn my son into a felon. You're such a good guy. What next? Do you want to sell him some weed too?"

Curtis laughed. *Sell him some weed? Hasn't Clyde noticed the kid doesn't have a job and seems to always have money?*

"I've got it on my bench here in the work shop; pop by when you have some time and I'll give it to you."

"Will do, see ya later."

Curtis took a sip of coffee and dropped fifty cents into the "honour" jar.

CHAPTER TEN

John Christmas's soul passed through his skin and bones as effortless as the wind was now passing into his house through the west wall. John didn't feel his soul travel up through the ceiling and beyond the tree tops or even sink down into the underworld, for that matter. Instead, it transcended forward, almost like taking a physical step to a new location directly in front of him. The whiteness began to drift pass like the rolling morning mist. Gradually, the shapes of large fir trees and the dimensions of a very old growth forest filtered into his senses.

John could feel the dampness of the ghost mist clinging to his thick hair. He could smell the ancient earth and the pungent essence of the heavy moss. John's peaceful soul knew that his body lay broken and dying in that dimensional step behind him. He didn't care; he felt no rush to go anywhere. He knew this forest was the sacred land of the elders, and he wanted to stay. As quietly and as nonintrusive as the shifting mist, a large black bear drifted in between the trees. His spirit could sense the massive being was older than the forest itself. And more majestic.

The bear did not walk directly to John. Instead, it led him to a nearby stream. Standing on the opposite side of the flowing water, the massive bear stared directly at John. Its large eyes looked like spot lights capturing John's soul, calculating and tallying up the deeds of his life.

"Suwinu (The Seer), do you know who I am?" the bear asked.

John remembered the ancient teachings clear in his mind. "Yes, you are Muin, my Spirit Guide. But you called me Suwinu; my name is John Christmas."

"You have been named before you were born. Suwinu — The Seer — is who you are. John Christmas was the name your false culture has labeled you," the bear lectured.

"Have you come to guide me to my elders?"

"No Suwinu. Your time for the Sacred Forest has not come… yet. Patience. Instead, you have been honoured by Kji Nestak as a guardian and warrior.

You are going to meet other warriors. A great and primordial evil is coming. Now, drink from the Sabáwe Cheboocheech (Sacred Stream).

As John (or Suwinu — The Seer) approached the stream, he thought of skipping over the water and standing on the other side beside the Muin.

The Great Bear curled back his lips and bellowed out a roar. The Sabáwe Cheboocheech instantly flared up its serene water into a turbulent deluge and doubled its width. Tension filled the ancient forest; massive arcs discharged between the trees like violent bolts of electricity climbing between the coils within a Nikola Tesla experiment.

"Do not play with me, young Suwinu. You do not yet belong on this side."

John couldn't help but feel like a child being scorned by a parent and immediately felt shame burn his cheeks.

Slowly, the Cheboocheech receded back to its original size. John stood there, too embarrassed to move. The intensity of the bear's eyes relaxed and calmness returned to the sacred forest.

"Come, young warrior," the Muin coaxed. "Renew yourself."

John stepped closer and knelt at the edge of the stream. The moon glistened and sparkled along the surface of the sacred water like diamonds under a jeweler's eye loupe. As John dipped his cupped hand into the water, he was transfixed as his mortal senses tried to process and understand the ethereal liquid flowing through his fingers. He rubbed his thumb and forefinger together as if lost in deep thought. His hand didn't *feel* wet — rather, it felt refreshed, replenished, clean.

Instinctively, John cupped the other hand and scooped a bowl of the Sabáwe Cheboocheech up to his lips. As the sacred water entered his mouth, he felt it washing down his throat, cleansing his mind and his entire being.

In sheer exhilaration, he cupped the stream again, rubbing his face, his hair and the back of his neck. He felt the piercing intensity of the water as it streamed down his chest and back.

He didn't just feel refreshed; he felt renewed. He felt *reborn.*

As John knelt there beside the stream, his soul vibrated. He felt bigger and better than before. He felt connected to the Cheboocheech, felt its endless flow, as if by consuming the sacred water he had become part of it and vice versa.

Slowly, John opened his eyes. The white mist rolled in towards him, separating him from the forest and the Muin.

"Be prepared, Suwinu," the Great Bear said from somewhere beyond John's sight. "Your world will once again need a warrior."

As the white blanket began to fade, John realized he was laying on his back staring at the domed light inside of the ambulance. He felt the raw burning of the breathing tube deep in his throat followed by the intense searing pain in his chest and back.

"He's coming around," he heard the paramedic cry.

The medic passed a pen light over each pupil to test their responsiveness. "Holy shit! His eyes are blue!"

CHAPTER ELEVEN

At five to six p.m., Curtis pulled into the parking lot of the Dartmouth Plaza where the Vietnamese restaurant was located. Lin's Wok was a small eatery that sat about 35 people and was tucked discreetly between a bank and a used sports equipment store. Curtis took a deep breath and pulled open the glass door and looked around. There were four numbered pictures of Lin's combination platters hanging on the wall. A ceramic Buddha sat on the counter near the cash register next to a small, open bowl of pink mint candies and the rest of the room was filled with Chinese decorations that Curtis was certain came from the Dollar Store at the other end of the plaza.

Curtis spied Eavery and Jerry sitting in the corner. They had pulled two tables together — an obvious indication there were more coming. Curtis stood staring at Eavery a second before taking a step towards them. Eavery still looked as he remembered him from yesterday (plain), but looking back at Jerry, Curtis realized this 'aura thing' was something he was going to have to get used to. He didn't see anything unusual on the drive over here. And he probably could have easily talked himself out of ever seeing anything to begin with, but as he stood in the diner — a room filled with cheap plastic dragons and hanging 3-D paper lanterns — hearing the background buzz of the fluorescent lighting his reality was cemented.

Eavery, too, was taken aback at the sight of Curtis. This new Curtis, with his almost white radiance — looked more confident, and stronger. Perhaps even taller, although Eavery wasn't sure if that was even physically possible. More likely it was that Curtis's abrupt change appeared to manifest a visual impact on him.

I don't know; he is different.

Curtis sat down and ordered a tea. He always ordered a tea in Asian restaurants as though he almost felt obligated. When Curtis looked up to make sure the waitress received his order correctly, he noticed that she was on older Vietnamese woman who, like them, was radiating. She was bathed in light orange, and she was staring at him with her mouth agape.

"Thank you. Just the tea," Curtis said again and leaned forward hoping she would take the hint.

"Very good, tea, very good," she mumbled. She quickly turned and sped to the kitchen, and before the door swung closed they could all hear her speaking excitedly in her native tongue.

The guys laughed to themselves as the cook, her husband, returned and was looking at Curtis through the serving window.

"Wow! Curtis, you have changed a lot since yesterday. Anything exciting happen to you last night?" Eavery asked.

Curtis filled them in on what happened at the boardwalk.

"Holy fucking shit! Jophiel? A fucking Cherubim? No fucking way?" Jerry said in amazement.

"No," Eavery corrected. "*THEE* fucking Cherubim. Their prince, the most powerful Cherubim; that would explain your glow." It hadn't occurred to Curtis that he too had a visible aura — after all, in the mirror, he still looked the same.

Just then three guys came and sat down at their table: Brent Martin, Angus Maclean and John Christmas (who Jerry introduced as Jack Frost).

Brent had a purple aura. He was a tall, lean man of thirty-six. His face was thin and deeply suntanned with a large bent, protruding nose. He was wearing a beige-collared Mountain Equipment Co-op gulf shirt that looked one size too small and too short for his frame, and khaki shorts that revealed his tendonous runners legs.

Angus also had a purple aura around him. He was an older round man in his late sixties who had the physical appearance of someone ten years older, but the energy of a man half his age. His moustache/goatee combo was whiter than his graying head and trimmed meticulously neat, but his evening's five o'clock shadow had come in heavy. Although it was nearing summer, Angus wore a navy blue turtleneck shirt, a black windbreaker with an embroidered stone tower on the left breast that said "Fort Louisburg Nova Scotia," and faded blue jeans.

Curtis looked at John (or Jack), for several seconds; he found him difficult to read. His aura seemed to fluctuate; it was almost like looking through a kaleidoscope. He was a strong and fit twenty-five year old. His hair was midnight black and cut short in a respectable business fashion. He wore a black t-shirt that read: *I should have took the BLUE pill*, and a long, black nylon trench coat, which Curtis assumed was meant to resemble the coat Neo wore in the *Matrix* trilogies. He had on dark grey suit slacks with black and white high-top running shoes. John had a 'Medicine Wheel' tattooed on the left side of his neck; the circle was two inches in diameter and was divided into four quadrants. Each quadrant represents a race of man and a direction. The line extending from the center travelling up (north) was black, the line extending east was white, the line running south was yellow, and the line extending west was red. What struck Curtis particularly odd were John's bright *blue* eyes. Each of the men took their turns staring at Curtis, then at Eavery and Jerry, and then back to Curtis again. As they were introduced, it was obvious they weren't quite sure what to make of each other.

After finally getting his tea, Curtis poured it into his little China tea cup and let it cool. "What is up with that?" Curtis said and pointed through the large bay window to the golden fog rolling high above Halifax.

"That, bye," Angus said revealing a strong Cape Breton accent, "is Elohim City."

"It's where the angels live," Eavery finished.

"What? I though angels live in heaven?" Curtis asked.

"No, the bible says they fly *up* to the heavens, which is antique talk for the *sky*," Jerry added.

"So why is it that I can see Elohim City right there, just hovering over Halifax?"

Angus looked back up at the golden city. "Because a high focus of divine energy rests there. In the *Sumerian Book of the Beginning*, which was later rewritten as the *Book of Genesis*, it reads that God breathed life on the earth where land meets water."

Jack added, "There is great spiritual energy at these points, specifically where the great oceans and continents meet. Halifax, like New York, Vancouver and L.A., have a high divine focus. That's why you can find the angel cities there."

Brent looked over at Jack like he just discovered electricity. "Los Angeles is the City of Angels and it literally has an angel city right above it. I never caught that before."

The look of shear disappointment on Jack's face made everyone at the table laugh out loud.

Jerry put down his miniature cup of tea and recomposed the conversation. "And humankind, who is also partly divine, is attracted to these locations. On a conscious level, you may like Halifax because of the fresh Atlantic air, or the lobster, but these divine focal points caress your spirit; they comfort you and you feel closer to the Creator."

"What about cities in the desert? Are there any angel cities there?" Curtis asked.

This time Angus answered, "God's divine breath passed along the coastal regions of earth; the interior of the continents were void of it. The result is a divine vacuum."

"The desert is the land of the Jinn," Jack added.

"The Jinn?" Curtis asked, a little shocked. "As in the demons from the Qur'an?"

"The Jinn are creatures that are neither angels nor demons, but are more like mischievous spirits," Eavery said.

"But deserts are beautiful. They are full of wildlife and nature, and First Nations people claim them to be holy places."

The old waitress, who was replenishing the previous tea pot with a fresh one, joined the conversation. "The native people, not just in North America, but also in South America, Australia, and around the world still hold their divinity close to the surface of their mind and heart. Long ago they were given charge of the *nether* regions to bless them and keep them blessed, and to hold the Jinn at bay. But as foreign beliefs and forces have mingled and distracted the natives or the "watchers," the Jinn have been getting stronger and more brazen. Even angry for being confined and held down," the waitress said in a vibrant Vietnamese-English.

Never hearing of the Jinn before tonight, Brent asked, "So what can they do?"

Jerry turned to Brent. "They distract the people who dwell in those regions from the divine connection. The Jinn can spread their immorality, contaminating the area to the point that will allow demons to enter."

Curtis envisioned a large split in the Nevada desert with flames shooting up and demons crawling out right before the "Welcome to Las Vegas" sign.

He had to check himself for a moment. This topic is getting really far out there; if a stranger was listening to even a little bit of what they were saying, he would automatically assume they had formed some kind of occult. Angels, demons — what next? Biblical Armageddon?

Eavery watched Curtis closely. Curtis had taken in a lot of information in such a short period of time; very soon he will need a breather to let him collect himself and absorb the new info.

"Curtis, can you give me a lift home? I took the bus out here," Eavery asked.

"Sure, I gotta head out anyways," Curtis replied.

Jerry looked over at Angus and Jack. "Okay, well… we'll have to get together again. Maybe over a few beers?"

"Yeah, like last time," Jerry nodded.

"We closed this place," Brent added with pride.

Angus shook his head, "This place closes at nine, bye. Not really anything to feel too proud `bout. Now, there is this one time that I can barely remember in Nor Sydney, me buddy Francis — he's a Newfie — got into me uncle's moonshine and for three days…"

"Angus, Angus, we have already heard all about you and your boyfriend Francis." Jerry broke in.

"He's me buddy, you sonavabitch. Why we ever joined you *bluenosers* is beyond the likes of me. You take me word, the Cape Breton Liberation Front will have us back as our own island again I tells ya, Jesus bye!"

"Thanks, Jerry! He's my ride home," Brent said holding his hands up.

Everybody laughed again at the table and Curtis and Eavery stood up.

"How much for the tea?" Curtis asked the waitress.

"No, no. Tea free," she said waving off his attempts of paying. "We must stick together, watch each other's back."

She reached out slowly and touched his shoulder. She

half expected to feel some little static charge or energy flow. Instead, what she felt was a deep pulse, like the resonating hum from the engines of a plane that are too low to hear but you can feel it deep in your core.

"Umm, thank you, then," Curtis said looking uncomfortably to others for support.

"There is an ancient spirit guiding that man," John said as the group watched Curtis exit out the small eatery.

As Curtis crossed over the bridge, he looked up into the golden mist of Elohim City far above his head. It seemed more solid when he was directly underneath of it. He turned to Eavery. "Lin seemed pretty adamant that we all stick together."

Eavery tried to brush off Curtis's concern. "Well there are a lot of dangers out there. It's good to have friends to rely on."

"That's true," Curtis responded, "There is that *everyday* fear of getting mugged, or being hit by a bus, but she seemed scared of something else. Is there something you're not telling me?"

Curtis became instantly aware of the tension building up in Eavery. Finally, he turned toward Curtis.

"Yes there is. I didn't know the right time to tell you, but..."

Curtis was watching Eavery the best he could and drive at the same time. The streetlights danced shadows across his face, making it impossible to accurately read his expression. Eavery was blatantly stalling and Curtis was beginning to get anxious.

"Curtis, you're not ready for it yet. You shouldn't get involved."

Curtis's heart skipped a beat.

Shouldn't get involved! I'm already involved. The things I've heard and seen recently — she could be talking about literally anything. That lady was pretty worked up and now Eavery didn't even want to talk about it.

Curtis's palms started to sweat and he repositioned his grip on the steering wheel.

"Eavery, seriously, if there is some tough shit coming my way — I need to prepare for it."

"Okay, you're right." Eavery said and shifted in his seat. "How is your Latin?"

"My Latin?" Curtis questioned, and then thought about it for a second. "Actually, good."

Curtis's answer caught Eavery off guard. "It is? You can speak Latin?"

"Yeah!" Curtis replied, also surprised by the fact.

"Did they teach you that in the military?"

"No, I just thought of Latin and it came to me."

"And you couldn't speak Latin until I asked you?"

Curtis had to think back. This was weird. Did he know Latin yesterday? He didn't think so. Who the hell learns Latin except for priests? But he couldn't remember not knowing it; it was if he just never tried it before. "I — I don't think so."

"Say something."

"*Quispiam.*"

Eavery blinked in surprise. "What did you say?"

"I said — *something.*"

"Really funny!"

"I must have got that ability from Jophiel. Why should I need Latin?" Curtis asked thinking back to Eavery's original question.

Eavery was lost in his thoughts of what else Jophiel may have transferred to Curtis. As far as he knew, no one else had the Cherubim ancestry. It was the Archangels who did most of the screwing around like Michael and Uriel. There was one guy, Gomez, from Chile, who had a connection with Camael, the prince of the Order of Powers. That boy was freaky. He knew and saw stuff no one else could. And the Order of

Powers was only two above the Order of Archangels, but four orders below the Cherubim.

"Latin, Eavery?" Curtis spat out, still anxious about the up and coming doom. "What would I need Latin for?"

Eavery snapped out of his thoughts. "What? Oh, to read the Old Testament. It's more powerful read aloud in Latin."

"More powerful? Why would it need to be more powerful?"

"Listen, Curtis, every Halloween the Wiccan covens from all around the eastern seaboard get together and conjure up Satan from the bowels of hell, and we literally have to send him back."

The colour drain from Curtis's face.

"*What the fuck*?" Curtis could barely get it out. This was far worse than he expected. "Holy shit! Satan? Actual Satan? I gotta pull over."

The car started to slow down and a honk came from behind. That was all Eavery could take and he started to roar with laughter.

"What? You're laughing?" Slowly it dawned on Curtis that he had just been had.

"Okay, okay, you should have seen your face," Eavery said still laughing. "This is a little off topic, but have you ever thought of Satan as an actual angel?"

"No, not really."

"Satan's angelic name is *Ha-Sata*, the Accuser. And his angelic duty was to travel throughout the earth and scrutinize the loyalty or dishonesty of humankind. Can you imagine only knowing humankind in that manner and being told to kneel down to them as *your* superior? No wonder he couldn't do it."

Curtis blinked. "Did you just take Satan's side?"

"No, of course not — it's just he *was* an angel and his duty for God built contempt; it seems like a pretty predictable outcome. Don't you think God would have had some kind of foresight? What that might create?"

Curtis could see Eavery's point—kinda, but since Curtis was raised Catholic, he had always seen Satan, or *Ha-Sata*, as the bad guy. Viewing Satan as a victim was new for him. Unsure what to make of Eavery's question, Curtis just shrugged his shoulders, "I guess so."

CHAPTER TWELVE

Las Vegas, Nevada

Fred dashed the last bit of salt on the large bowl of freshly popped popcorn. After working twelve days straight at the casino, he was looking forward to his one night off. With dozen bottles of Bud Light and a joint, he planned on chilling out tonight.

"Hurry up honey!" A call came from the other room.

"I'm coming! Go ahead and hit play."

Samantha, or Sam, as her friends called her, extended her arm and hit play on the remote. Fred sat down next her as the trailers for up-and-coming movies began to play. Julian, their two year old Jack Russell terrier began to growl.

"Quiet boy!"

Fred threw him a piece of popcorn. The dog ignored it; instead he began barking at the corner of the ceiling on the opposite side of the room.

Sam looked over at Julian and rubbed his back, "It is okay boy, shhh."

She noticed that the dog was very tense and ridged. He sprung from the sofa and darted over to the corner of the room, erupting into vicious barking.

"Holy shit, Sam! Why don't you toss that mutt outside. I think he needs to take a piss."

Sam got up cautiously. "Maybe someone's outside. Look at him; he's flipping out."

As she crossed the room she noticed that that corner of the ceiling was darker than the rest of the room, as if she was already casting a shadow, but the light was still in front of her.

With the terrier in hysterics, Fred put the bowl down on the coffee table. "Does it look like somebody is outside? Should I grab the gun?"

Almost to the corner now, Sam slowed her approach. The hair on her arms straightened up and she felt a primitive tingle run down her spine. Staring into the shaded corner she felt as if she was standing on the cusp of a deep well. Cold. Bottomless.

Terrified, she held her gaze to the shapeless shadow.

"Come... on... boy... Come here." Fear was tight in her throat.

The dog began to whine and then bark again in defiance.

"What is going on over there?" Fred asked as he pulled his Smith and Wesson Sigma 9mm handgun out of the end table.

"We have to get out of this house, Fred." Sam managed to say. Finally her *flight* response was having her take small steps back. As Fred stepped closer, the terrier's loyalty and protective instincts rose and his verbal assault on the shadow increased.

Samantha was taking quick shallow breaths. "There is something evil in that corner. We... have to leave... right now."

Using his gun as an extended finger, Fred pointed into the corner. "What is that?"

Sam continued taking short steps backwards. "I don't

know, but can't you feel it? It's evil: a poltergeist or ghost or something. Back away Fred; even the dog is warning you."

Fred looked down at Julian. The terrier looked rabid with foam frothing in his mouth and an aggression he had never witnessed in the pet before. Fred could sense something wasn't right, but with the solid weight of the weapon in his hand he felt he could handle whoever was still in the backyard. Stepping closer to the corner, Fred's evolutionary sixth sense — the survival attribute that humans have mostly lost touch with — had sprung to life and he could now feel the distinct presence of evil. He could tell the corner was darker than it should be, but that didn't alarm him. He was trapped in the mindset that the danger was outside.

"Fred, what the hell are you doing? Get your ass away from the corner. Can't you see it up there?"

Leaning even closer Fred was squinting to try to make out some kind of form. He stretched out his arm and began probing the corner with the snub barrel of his gun.

"Sam is this ever weird. It's like a black mist, and it's cold."

A whine came from Julian at his feet. Fred looked down as the small terrier began to whimper and yelp. Both Fred and Samantha watched in horror as the dog's head tilted back and his jaws began to open wide. Screaming in agony, its small paws were trying to back pedal out of the corner but instead were only sliding on the wooden floor. Blood began trickling out of the corners of his mouth, and with a large *crack* the terrier's jaw was torn from his body and dropped to the floor. In a moment's freedom, but blind with pain, the dog bolted from Fred's feet and ran around the room crashing into the walls and legs of furniture before running into an open closet door to hide.

"*OH MY GOD!*" Sam screamed at the torture her Julian just endured. With the beginning of hysterics setting in, she turned her gaze from the closet back to Fred. "What the... what the... what the fuck just happened?" she stammered.

Fred's mouth hung open and his throat was dry. "I... don't... I don't know." He sputtered confused.

But then he felt it: the fear. It was the kind of fear that humans have forgotten about after thousands of years being on the top of the food chain. Fred felt the ancient, unadulterated sensation of terror that all living beings feel when they realize their life is about to be torn away from them. He slowly turned and looked at Samantha; her eyes were fixed on the ceiling, and her mouth was gaping open as if releasing a silent scream. Slowly her left hand rose and she shakily pointed in his direction. Fred couldn't even turn to look; fear had struck him completely motionless. Tears were streaming out of his eyes as he stared at her. The strength and courage that he received earlier from his Smith and Wesson was now gone; it only felt heavy and useless. He let it slip from his fingers, falling to the floor with a solid thud.

His pulse raced and he lost his breath as what felt like one thousand cold, damp micro-fingers caressed the far side of his body. Samantha watched as the dark shadow took shape into a fibrous, black mold-like form. She watched Fred staring back at her. They were both physically locked with fear, and neither of them were able to move. Fred stood there crying, stiff as a mannequin on display in a window. A puddle of urine soaked his socked feet and the front of his jeans. She watched as the dark creature's eyes pierced yellow and a smile formed on a fabric-like face.

A rattling gurgle came from the demon's throat. Slowly, black fibrous wings stretched out behind the creature. Tears began to pour out of Samantha's eyes as a roar that vibrated the foundation of their house was released from the demon. Just then, Fred turned to see the creature for the first time, causing his bowels to release into his pants. There is no description of the terror that penetrated every cell in his body.

A half second before Fred's heart stopped, the demon plunged his hand through Fred's chest; the hand exited his back in a gruesome explosion of blood, bone and flesh, grasping eight inches of spine. Within that final moment before Fred's death, time stopped. Fred could feel the unquantifiable pain from the violent violation of the demon's hand and forearm entering his body. The pain was so intense that Fred wanted the release of death, wanted the comfort of it. He waited for it. And he waited. Deep coldness engulfed his body, and a billion distant screams filled his ears. He looked into the creature's face.

Why? Surely, I must be dead by now. The pain — Ohhh, the pain! Why do I still feel the pain?

"Because I can make this last an eternity. Time holds no authority over me, Freddy," the demon gurgled, answering Fred's thoughts.

As Fred stared into the demon's face; it's mouth didn't move but he knew it was talking to him. With another roar, the demon's wings stretched over Fred's body; clawed hands on the tip of the wings grabbed Fred's shoulders. Slowly, they pulled Fred in two like the tearing of a paper doll. Fred knew he should already be dead, but he could still feel his body being torn, his bones snapping. Screaming for mercy, Fred felt the last of his body give way.

Finally, blackness, and death. But the pain was still there.

How can there still be pain — -Ohhh, the pain!

He could feel himself fall — not to the floor, but deeper, much deeper. The screams were getting louder. *The pain — Ohhh, the pain!* In the darkness Fred began to see something — light, yes, light.

God please take me. End my suffering. That's not light. That's fire! NOOOOOOOOO!

Samantha watched as the demon ate Fred's body. Still frozen in fear, she followed the yellow eyes as they fixed themselves on hers. A bloody smile rose across its face. The demon dropped Fred's clothes and gracefully floated across the floor toward her. Its fibrous teeth gave dimension to its mouth. Crying, Samantha couldn't move; she could only stand there as the demon's teeth engulfed her face.

Pierre-Elliott Trudeau International Airport, Montréal, Canada

Flying back into Canada was not something Lukács was looking forward to, but he had never questioned the Vezető before. The driver was over one hour late picking him up from the airport due to various detours and road closures. Montréal always seemed to be under some kind of construction.

Don't they ever finish fixing this city?

Finally on his way, Lukács watched as the familiar lights of St. Catherine Street passed by.

The black Lincoln Continental waited as the gated doors to the private driveway automatically opened. A large stone plaque, edged in brass, read Hungarian Canadian Chamber of Commerce, 4144 Dorchester Blvd., identified the conservative building. The chamber of commerce is a very successful link between Hungarian and Canadian businesses; it is also the KRÁJCÁR's North American central office and is commonly referred to as the *Embassy.*

With the large red, white and green colours of the Hungarian flag waving from a pole secured above a stone archway, Lukács stepped out of the car and was greeted by a fellow Magyar.

"Bonjour, Lukács. Welcome to Montreal," Khagan said as he leaned forward to give him a kiss on both cheeks and paused when he neared a bandage.

"Oh, yes, Almod," he said looking off to the side. "A great brother, he will be missed."

Khagan Szalai was the head associate at the Embassy and the son of the KRÁJCÁR's second in command, Elek Szalai.

He studied international business and foreign relations at Budapest's prestigious Corvinus University. Khagan has always showed respect towards Lukács with maybe a slight playful intonation (resembling sibling rivalry), but there was something Lukács just didn't like about him. Maybe it was his cinnamon cologne or his Armani suits. He knew Khagan was the business face of the KRÁJCÁR, supplying millions of dollars for their causes; Lukács's own expenses weren't cheap. But Khagan just seemed like a pencil neck to him. Maybe deep down Lukács knew that Khagan was higher on the food chain and he resented him for it. Even now they weren't equals, and Khagan had a much better chance of sitting at the table within the Group of Seven than he did.

"What is the matter Khagan? Do you lack the constitution for tradition? Or was Almod not that *great* of a brother?"

Walking down a polished marble hallway, Lukács followed Khagan into his office. There along the many shelves were pictures of Khagan shaking hands with Premiers, Prime Ministers, and there was even a large framed photo of Khagan toasting a beer with President Barack Obama at a fundraiser in Toronto.

Khagan gracefully floated around his desk and sat down. After pulling out a folder and sliding it across his cherry wood desk, he cupped his hands and studied Lukács.

"This was initially Almod's assignment."

"Zo I've heard."

Lukács opened the folder and flipped through half a dozen pictures of a man in his mid-thirties. The pictures showed the man leaving work, crossing the street, standing next to his wife and child; there were notes of his work timetable and home address — the standard intelligence.

"He's a little old to have just popped up out of nowhere; I hope your men aren't slipping," Lukács said with a hint of disapproval in his tone.

Khagan ignored his remark. "We believe he had just

recently changed; it is uncommon but it does happen from time to time."

Closing the folder Lukács's gaze fixed on a framed five foot painting of Attila the Hun mounted directly behind Khagan's desk. Historians believe that Attila's flattened oblong skull was formed by wrapping bandages around his infant head while the plates of the skull were still soft. Lukács, however, grew up being told that Attila's deformation was caused from being struck by the "Sword of God" from the Archangel Caviel to test him. Although it deformed Attila, his ability to withstand such a blow proved to God that Attila was worthy of the task bestowed upon him. And within the brotherhood, the tradition of wrapping was created and was carried on throughout the Hun ancestry, right up to the modern day KRÁJCÁR leader Gergõ Mátyás.

"I vill need a car." Lukács stated flatly.

"I had the Audi brought around to the front, and your effects are presently being transferred over to it. A reservation has been made at the Lord Nelson on South Park Street, under Stephen McDonald." Khagan sat back in his Italian leather chair with a diminutive smile. He always took a little pleasure in putting Lukács in personally awkward positions.

"Do I zound like a McDonald?"

"Just show up in a kilt holding a bottle of *Pusser's Rum*; they will think you're from Newfoundland."

Lukács fished his tongue between his teeth in a display of discontent. "Baszik ön!"

Khagan's smile slid off his face. "Now that was inappropriate."

Lukács turned and walked out of the office with a smile of his own on his face.

CHAPTER THIRTEEN

Curtis pulled into the driveway of Lake View Apartments. With bulky pine trees landscaping the yard and a large grocery store plaza across the busy intersection, Curtis couldn't help but wonder where the view of the lake was.

"Thanks for the ride; you saved me two hours on the bus."

"Don't mention it. But you still haven't filled me in to what that Vietnamese lady was worried about," Curtis said.

Eavery shifted in his seat. "You're right. Shut the car off."

Curtis pulled forward into an empty "visitors only" parking spot.

"Lin was talking about the KRÁJCÁR. They are an ancient fraternity of self-righteous assholes who have taken it upon themselves to rid the world of the Nephilim."

"What do you mean by 'rid the world of'?"

"I'm talking about assassinating, killing, murdering the Nephilim. The last count I had, they have murdered five people in Canada this year and about thirty around the world."

The confusion was apparent on Curtis's face. "How do they even know who we are? And why would they want to kill us? And why haven't they been arrested or something?"

This wasn't the first time Eavery had been bombarded by

these questions. Over the last several years, Eavery had become the unofficial welcome wagon of the *recently changed*.

"Okay, okay! Firstly, they know who you are because they have their people in every city in every country in the world and they too can see the aura. We don't have a monopoly on aural perception. A lot of spiritual people can see us as we are. The Druids and the Hindus are very keen at it. The KRÁJCÁR believe they are ridding the world of Satan's children. They believe the Nephilim are the unnatural union of demons and humans and fifteen hundred years of fundamentalism and prejudice have walled up any chance of reasoning and clear thinking. And they do get caught every once in a while, but their assassins play the psycho-killer card ranting something about communism or Allah, or whatever is the new flavour of the day." The weight of the news was sinking in.

"Who exactly are these... what did you call them? Crashcars?"

"It's pronounced *croy-car*. They started in Hungary before Hungary was, well, Hungary. You know, to understand the KRÁJCÁR we have to go back to the beginning."

Eavery paused and collected his thoughts for a second.

"What am I in for? A history lesson?" Curtis snickered.

"No, you are in for *thee* history lesson."

Curtis let his snicker fade and steadied himself.

"I am talking about language — specifically angelic language — and even more specifically, Angelic Script: the divine language that angels and gods use to communicate with each other but in written form."

Curtis was a little shocked. He was expecting something along the lines of medieval Europe and the Catholic Church, not "angelic script."

Wait — did he just say gods?

Eavery continued. "Around 3700 B.C., the Egyptian god Thoth taught some lowly tribal priest hieroglyphic script, which was the foundation of the Angelic Script."

"The foundation? How do you mean?" Curtis asked.

"I mean the Angelic Script was taught in three levels over a thousand years."

"Why over a thousand years and not in ten years or all at once?"

"Well, for one, humankind was still in the Stone Age; they didn't house the mental fortitude for such advancement. And I can assume because they are divine, they probably knew what they were doing.

Try to remember, at this point in human history there was no written language at all, anywhere. So when Thoth introduced the primitive Egyptian priests to hieroglyphs, their brains must have hurt, kinda like cramming all night for an exam. And, at that point in history, their civilization exploded. Until the Romans under Alexander the Great, they dominated the world. By the way, the word hieroglyph means "divine language" in Egyptian, and "sacred script" in Greek."

Call it coincidence, but it was only a few days earlier that Curtis watched a documentary on the History Channel about this very topic.

"I thought the first written language was found in ancient Iraq," Curtis countered.

"It wasn't for another two hundred years, around 3500 B.C.. In Mesopotamia, which is now modern-day Iraq, Iran, Turkey, and Jordan, archeologists found pictures in clay called cuneiforms. These pictographs and logograms are pictures of, say, for example, a fish — which meant a fish or fishing. It was extremely crude and did little to advance the tribes. But by this point, the Egyptians had already invented the sail for their boats and were mapping the Mediterranean, and were developing the upper and lower sections of the Nile River. But for those two hundred years, the Egyptians used a form of cursive hieroglyphic script where they wrote on papyrus and leather in order to teach it to other tribes. They styled it in a Rebus format, a multitude of pictures creating a single thought. For instance, you might find a picture or *ideogram* of an eyeball, a bumblebee, and a leaf. They are three distinct pictures but together they form the thought: "I bee-lieve." Simple, sure, but light years ahead of the competition. By 3100 B.C., Thoth appeared again for a second lesson to a man named *Meni*. He taught Meni to etch the script into stone, and where the initial cursive script was sloppy — albeit effective — this new technique, known as Middle Egyptian, was very complicated even by today's standards. Thoth introduced *phonograms* — sound writing — and *determinatives*, which I won't bother getting into here in the car, but the script was written right to left and in columns top to bottom."

"So, this Meni was a priest then?" Curtis asked, fascinated and drawn into the topic.

Eavery watched Curtis as he hung onto every word like a child captivated by the mystifying performance of a magician.

"No, he was just some common man. He must have showed some promise though; he became Egypt's first pharaoh, King Menes. He united Upper and Lower Egypt into one country and founded the city of Memphis as its capital. This catapulted Egypt into the most powerful nation on earth.

As the Egyptians expanded their territory and began trading goods with distant cultures, the knowledge of the Angelic Script also spread, mostly as the result of doing business but also because of ego — an 'I'm-smarter-than-you' kind of thing. It is very easy to see the rise of these foreign civilizations when you compare them to known Egyptian trade routes. Thoth declared the Egyptians his own people and he ordered them to keep the sacred knowledge secret, but down through the generations greed outweighed the accord between the first Egyptians and Thoth."

"So what did he do?" Curtis asked, envisioning Eavery's story as narrated documentary.

"There was nothing he could do. Once man is given knowledge of something, it cannot be taken away; he must give it up freely. That is a code declared by the Creator himself. There isn't an angel in existence who would try to break that law, not even Ha-Sata. Not that he would; he loves what we are doing to ourselves. He even helped the knowledge along."

That last comment struck Curtis oddly.

"Satan helped us gain knowledge? Like what, the forbidden apple in the Garden of Eden?" Curtis toyed.

CHAPTER FOURTEEN

Ballina, Ireland

Jennifer Leary was finally leaving Ireland for her first exotic retreat. She finished tying her long red hair into a tight pony-tail and swung it over her left shoulder. Her hair wasn't naturally this colour red, it required some professional help, but tourists expected the Irish country-side to be green, it's rainbows to end in gold, and of course, their lassies to be red heads.

What the hell.

Just about to turn thirty-one she was flying out of Dublin's International Airport, enroute to Cairo, to celebrate the Summer Solstice in the shadows of the Great Pyramids of Giza.

She couldn't wait to leave the banging from the construction of the new casino-slash-adult entertainment lounge being built across the road, although it will bring in a lot of new business for the pub she manages and for the town of Ballina, but it is going to change the whole feel of this sleepy little fishing village.

In the last two years, Jennifer's life had changed dramatically. After seeing a flyer posted on the community wall about a new Wiccan movement in the small village of Kells, she quickly went from a non-practicing Protestant to a fully-involved Wiccan priestess. There was something very appealing about its ancient heritage and simplistic convictions that drew her in. Through them she met her boyfriend Liam, gave up the booze (for the most part), and went from waitressing at the pub to managing it.

Jennifer gets insulted whenever someone declares modern Wicca to be only a "romantic" version of what witchcraft, or even druidry, once was. And she hates it when ignorant people called it "devil worship" or paganism, as if Christianity was somehow more benevolent or realistic.

As she finished packing her suitcase, she placed her *athame*, or ceremonial double-edged dagger, and her wand in the center and folded her hooded robe on top of them. Unfortunately, airport security would never allow her to carry the ceremonial blade on board. In Wiccan practices, the athame is never used to cut anything physical; if it does the metal is considered tainted. Instead, it is used to cast a circle or cleanse and empower items. Looking over at her altar, Jennifer watched as the last flicker of the white candle went out.

Just in time.

Jennifer could feel a cold, bitter breeze hitting the back of her neck, like a late autumn wind. The fine, tiny hairs on her neck stood straight up and Jennifer felt as if someone was standing behind her. She quickly turned around and found the room exactly how it should be — empty.

I must have left a window open.

Reaching into the warm wax of the candle, she pulled out a small charm in the shape of a fish. She instantly felt better once she placed the talisman on a gold chain and locked the clasp around her neck. The symbol of the fish, which as many meanings, represents the Archangel Raphael who is the patron and protector of travelers.

She placed her heavy suitcase on the floor, extended its telescopic handle, and then reaching for her travel bag, which contained some essentials — fresh underwear, socks and a t-shirt — just in case her suitcase was sent to Chicago and not Cairo, she started for the front door.

Oh crap!

Scurrying back to her bedroom altar she grabbed a lone scarlet pimpernel wildflower and placed it into her pocket. Next to the flower was a small 2 ½ cm copper pentagram broach that she pinned to her left breast pocket on her jacket.

The pentacle, or pentagram (a five-pointed star encased in a circle), represents good luck and has been found on bits of potter and clay coins dating back to 4000 B.C. in the Euphrates-Tigris region (modern day Iraq and Iran).

Two weeks earlier during the last full moon, Jennifer performed an Empowering Jewelry Protection spell on her broach. She sat within her magic circle and cleansed and consecrated her pentacle with the four elements (earth, wind, water and fire) and chanted seven times:

Formed in Earth and forged in Fire
Goddess blessing, lift me higher
Guard me from life's evil blows
Please make sure my safety grows
Goddess grant me my desire
Formed in Earth and forged in Fire

This spell blesses the jewelry and protects the wearer from evil and harm.

Jennifer checked to make sure all the windows in her apartment were closed, grabbed her keys and walked out the front door. Although the hallway is well-lit, anxiety crept into the pit of her stomach. Fear and dread fingered its way up her spine. Locking the bolt on her door, she looked up to the *wedjat eye*, or the Eye of Horus, painted above the frame.

Jennifer began to sense a very old evil behind her in the hall. The McMullans in 2A were never home this time of day, and the O'Deas in 2C were gone to London on vacation so there was no one to hear her scream for help if she needed to. Adjusting the travel bag over her shoulder, she swallowed hard and grabbed the small enchanted fish around her neck and softly prayed to the Archangel Raphael.

Then, as if a wall had been placed behind her, she could no longer feel the penetrating stare and ancient coldness that had almost literally stopped her dead. With strength and conviction she turned around and faced the small landing before the stairs. A part of her sensed the evil was still there, watching her, wanting her, but she also sensed a powerful force protecting her, shielding her. As she took her first step down the stairs, she stopped and looked over her right shoulder. She felt a flood of joy and relief wash over her and a melting of the evil zephyr that gripped her only seconds earlier.

"Thank you, Raphael," she muttered and walked down the stairs and into the waiting taxi.

Raphael stood at the top of the stairs, his brass and alabaster marbled skin churned with intensity and his wings outstretched wide, filling the landing. His arm had extended his brilliant sword into the chest of a black demon. A hissing and burning sound escaped the wound around the edges of the blade.

"It is time you return to your cave, Rossziel," Raphael charged, as he slowly raised his sword and easily sliced through the demon.

The torment on the demon's face twisted and distorted its already disgusting features. His wings spread wide in a surrendering pose, and his claws balled into a fist. Then, unexpectedly, the creature smiled.

"Go ahead and send me back home, cousin," the demon jeered. "The humans are defiling this soil." Looking over his shoulder, the demon pointed through the window to the construction across the road.

"Soon, many more of my brothers will come and take my place. You will never stop us all. We... will... own this town." The demon laughed aloud.

"There will be a battle for this town, *cousin*, but YOU will not be fighting it." Raphael raised his sword through the neck and face of the demon and watched it come out the top of his head. The demon's upper body split in two, its black and decayed innards oozed and dropped to the floor. Each half of his face smiled and watched the angel with its eye. Slowly, like black mist coming off of contaminated dry ice, the dark demon began to dissolve into the floor.

At the last second, Raphael pulled out a large shimmering dagger and pierced the hardened black core of the demon's exposed heart. With a thunderous scream, the creature exploded directly into the floor; the shriek blew the windows out of the stairway and glass door, and sent a crack through the wall and foundation of the apartment below.

CHAPTER FIFTEEN

Eavery recomposed his thoughts, "Okay, okay I went way off topic there. What was I talking about?" Eavery searched. "...knowledge, sacred script and how the Egyptians were spreading it all willy-nilly." Eavery followed his trail of thought back to where he left off.

"As Middle Egyptian spread, humankind's knowledge also expanded. Metallurgy, geometry, astronomy, astrology, mathematics, mummification... humankind exploded in its first cultural and intellectual enlightenment.

Around 2400 B.C., within the 4th Dynasty, the Egyptian Pharaoh Djedefre sent two of his sons, Atulekha and Lantis, off to establish Egyptian colonies as trading ports in the Mediterranean Sea. These two princes formed the Kefchu tribe. They founded Crete and Thera, or what today is called Santorini. It was also known as *Atlantis.*"

"Shut the fuck up! Atlantis is real? Are you messing with me?"

Eavery always got a kick out of people's reactions when he told them that. "Of course it *was* real there is an excessive amount of evidence to prove that. Our problem today is that we believe we are at the top of our technological abilities and that this is the first time we ever invented our 'modern' gadgets. In our 2.5 million year history, that is a pretty narrow-minded view."

Atlantis, a 2.5 million year history... Curtis needed to know more.

"Okay, but the Minoans settled Crete and the Greeks settled Santorini," Curtis said.

"No, that's not true; the Minoan myth was coined after the archeologist Arthur Evans discovered the 5000 year old palace, Knossos, back in 1904. He tongue-in-cheekily called the ruler King Midas from the fairy tale. He had later acknowledged that it was a silly thing to do but he was the discoverer, and it stuck."

"So Atlantis was actually two islands?"

"The Egyptian-Kefchu colonies were several islands"

A lot of thoughts were running through Curtis's head. "But these 'Atlanteans' supposedly had an advanced utopia with flying machines and automobiles."

"They did. Archeologists have actually found three-storied homes with multiple bedrooms and bed frames still in them, indoor hot and cold running water, and an indoor toilet and sewer system."

Eavery could tell by Curtis's face he wasn't appreciating the magnitude of the technology. "Curtis, this was a *thousand* years before the Greek empire even existed! They were still living in one-level mud huts — never mind having an indoor bathroom."

Curtis blinked and tipped his head. "Wow!"

"Wow, yeah," Eavery added. "And that is actual evidence on display in the Santorini and Kamari museums. Now throw in an atomic blast, a 100-foot tsunami, and 80 feet of soot and ash. What you get is complete destruction of a small civilization. Do the same thing to, say, Prince Edward Island, and see what is left of Charlottetown."

"Did you say an atomic blast?" Curtis asked.

"Yes, an atomic blast over a very large super volcano; I guess with all their brains they weren't all that smart."

"Where did they get that technology from? Aliens?"

"No, Ha-Sata," Eavery answered flatly.

"Ha-Sata? Satan? Just like that? You're dropping in the Satan bomb?" Curtis played in an overly dramatic and sarcastic tone. The thought of Satan doing anything but playing the boogeyman (let alone offering up nuclear technology) seemed very absurd.

"Yep," Eavery played back. "Sounds a little too simple doesn't it?"

"Sounds a little too — Baptist. *I'm sorry Lord, Satan made me do it!*" Curtis said in a mocking southern preacher's tone.

Eavery laughed at his friend. "Sometimes the bad guys actually do bad shit. Who can say if he knew by advancing them a few thousand years technologically that it would destroy their civilization but, he is, after all, Satan."

Curtis rubbed his temples then popped the buckle securing his seatbelt. Sliding his seat back, he shifted in his seat to make it easier to look at Eavery dead on.

"Okay, so we have gods teaching nomadic priests a divine language — Angelic Script or something."

Eavery nodded. "Yes, that's right."

Curtis continued, "Then we have the creation of the Egyptian people and their country, the development of sciences, the invention of the sailboat, and the *rise* and *fall* of Atlantis. Did I forget anything? Oh, and a Satanic nuclear bomb that exploded over a super volcano, wiping out two ancient civilizations. Is that the gist of it?"

"So far," Eavery said, amused at Curtis's little rant.

"Then what the hell does all that have to do with the KRÁJCÁR?"

Eavery feigned an exhaustive sigh.

"If you would just let me finish, my young padawan. As

you may be aware, the Nephilim race came into being in 2314 B.C...."

"2314 B.C.?" Curtis interrupted. "That's pretty precise."

"Let's just say I can remember the event."

"Alright, we can say that," Curtis gave in.

Eavery gave another sigh, but this time with a smirk. "Before I was interrupted, I was saying that the KRÁJCÁR's ambition is to destroy the Nephilim because of their genetic divination; it helps the Nephilim to read and speak the pure Angelic Script."

"So what? The hieroglyphs are a dead language and literally thousands of Egyptian scholars can read it — there's got to be a million books on the subject."

"Yes, but Thoth only taught three of the four levels. He believed humans weren't yet ready for the fourth and final level: the full Angelic Script. The Egyptian god was waiting for another one thousand years for the puny human brain to adapt to the extraordinary knowledge."

"Is that when Satan stepped in?"

Eavery smiled and continued. "Ha-Sata wanted the new Kefchu nation to worship him. He wanted to become their new 'Ra,' their new sun god. So he taught them the fourth level: the full Angelic Script."

"And they made a bomb?" Curtis questioned, the long day was wearing his faculties a little thin.

"It corrupted them," Eavery continued, oblivious to Curtis's fatigue. "The more they knew, the more they wanted to know. They became addicted to knowledge. They increasingly answered the *how*s, the *why*s, and the *what*s. They never paused to question the *should*s."

Even though it was June, a cold blanket of fear nettled down and around Curtis and he shivered as the hairs on his arms stood erect.

Eavery's description of the Kefchu's (Atlantean's) lack of moral stewardship in guiding their technological abilities rang loud in Curtis's head because it resembled the world of today with its genetically modified crops, petroleum products, food factories, new weekly viral vaccines, and thousands of disorders that can be "fixed" by simply taking a pill. The world was spinning out of control and Curtis could imagine it ending in the same way as Atlantis — with a *bang*.

"So what is the fourth level? What was missing from the third?"

"Omniscience! The knowledge of everything."

What Eavery had just said hung heavy and made the air in the car thick and palpable. The weight of it compressed Curtis into his seat and made the world outside sound dull and listless; it felt as though he was under water.

"The Atlanteans didn't question their drive for knowledge or want for technology. At first, Ha-Sata achieved his goal: he became a powerful sun god. But after a few centuries, science replaced religion and technology blurred ethics. Soon everyone had the right to do anything. And in this utopia of unprecedented freedom, where every goal and achievement was only a step for the next goal, no one took any responsibility. In the end it destroyed them."

"And they took the fourth level with them, right? I mean, that blast destroyed everything — except a few homes that they are only now finding," Curtis said then added, "and you questioned me about not having a cell phone!"

Eavery unbuckled his seatbelt and propped open the door.

"Soon all of Santorini will be excavated. There are about to be some very big findings that will change what everyone thought they knew about the ancients. Buried on that island are museums, universities, laboratories... Soon it's going to happen all over again — but this time on a global scale."

Curtis felt like there must be something he was missing. Although this new revelation was dramatic and even potentially mind blowing, Curtis didn't see an apocalyptic ending.

"But nobody can read it. It's written in an unknown hieroglyph."

Eavery paused and looked at Curtis waiting for the light to click on in his head.

He still doesn't get it.

"You can," he said at last. "So can other Nephilim."

There was the light.

Curtis thought back to the documentary he watched on the *Discovery Channel*, and his ability to decipher the frescoes on Santorini about Susemon the fisherman, his wife the beautician and his three children.

"And," Eavery continued, "that is where the KRÁJCÁR come in." He swung the car door wide and stepped out. "Thanks for the lift home."

"What about the KRÁJCÁR? How do we stop them?"

It was too late; Eavery vanished into the darkened parking lot.

***

Curtis's head was filled with the unbelievable history lesson he received as he drove home. His imagination raced with future events of massive archeological discoveries followed by gigantic leaps in science and technology that would eventually lead to the fabled Armageddon. *Perhaps not so fabled after all.* He let his eyes wander up at the underside of the angel city. The thick, metallic golden clouds churned, forming some unrecognizable shape before reforming into something else.

How could I have not seen that city before?

He had to keep forcing himself to look back at the road. It was an awesome sight and it was hard to look away. It mesmerized him like snowflakes brushing pass the windshield during a snow storm. The oncoming lights and honking from a car snapped Curtis out of his daze. He didn't notice he had drifted into the other lane until he saw he had forced the oncoming traffic off the street and onto the grass of someone's front lawn.

Holy shit! "Sorry about that!" Curtis yelled out his window. With his heart pounding from the near miss he pulled his Accord back into his lane and tried to focus on the road. As he was approaching his street, he watched people going for walks in the fresh summer air. Some were walking their dogs and some were holding their cats. He noticed some of the people had a halo, or a *nimbus,* with a very slight coloured hue to it. That was odd — must be exhibiting a new genetic anomaly. By the time Curtis got in, Charlie was already fast asleep and Vivica was tucked in bed reading her novel.

"How did your date with Eavery go?"

"Oh, it went okay. He introduced me to a few of his friends. He asked me to drive him home so he didn't have to take the bus."

"You brought the car home this time, right? Cause I need to drive up to the university and start preparing for my trip. I am heading off in a couple of days, don't forget."

"I'm not forgetting," Curtis said taking off his watch and placing it on the dresser. "And look at you with the covers pulled up to your neck. You've gotta be sweating under there?"

"No, I'm not really wearing much," Vivica said as she rolled down the sheets and exposed a very lacy and very see-through pink teddy.

A large smile spread across Curtis's face and he quickly got undressed. "Now I see why you were waiting up for me. Looking that good, I'm surprised you didn't start without me," he said feeling a little overconfident.

Vivica reached up to turn off the light. "Who said I didn't?"

CHAPTER SIXTEEN

After such an athletic episode, Curtis would normally be in a deep sleep. But tonight his mind wouldn't let him rest. He dreamt he was in ancient Israel along the Jordan River. He didn't know how he knew it was ancient Israel, or the Jordan River, but his omnipresent conscience — the master of all dream weaving — filled in the blanks. Two men approached him through a lush green vineyard that spread along the riverbank and up the surrounding hills. They were walking between the rows with their hands out and their fingers brushing the vine leaves. The one on the right had a large, friendly smile on his face. He could tell the first man was Jophiel, although he didn't look like an angel at all; he wasn't black and silver or a giant. He didn't even have wings. He looked like a very average man of average height and weight. Curtis didn't know who the other man was, but the sun glistened off his skin the way it does off a freshly waxed surface. They both wore a brown and white robe with a leather belt and leather sandals, but Jophiel had his scroll fastened near his hip. The other man had a long sword in a polished gold scabbard.

"Hello Curtis! What a beautiful day," Jophiel commented as he came closer.

Curtis looked around and examined the surroundings. The sun was hot and intense and he could feel a refreshing coolness coming off the river.

"Is this a dream?" Curtis asked feeling a little apprehensive. He felt far too aware for it to be a dream.

"Yes it is," Jophiel said in a very jovial tone while still smiling.

The stranger didn't identify himself or even offer a hello; he just looked at Curtis with disinterest.

"Is this your dream or is it mine? It feels very real."

"It is your dream but it is my memory. This is one of my favourite times and places. It is a time of peace, and abundance in everything — a true golden age. It will be another thousand years before this land is claimed by the Hebrews. The Zamzummins are flourishing to the north, the Anakims are thriving to the south, and the Canaanites to the west are building their great cities. Our children are healthy and prospering."

Curtis looked around again; the land was beautiful and the soil looked dark and rich. Off into the distance he could see the shoreline of the Sea of Arabah, which was to become the *Dead Sea* (before three thousand years of evaporation and heavy agricultural use of its rivers). It looked much larger in the dream than it actually does in the present day.

Jophiel's mood was already infecting Curtis; he could feel the smile spread across his lips. "I understood angels don't talk to humans much, I must be your favourite one," Curtis said a little cocky.

"It is true that I have taken a liking to you, human. You may consider yourself honoured." Jophiel tried to drop his smile while he spoke, but it crept back in spite of himself.

Curtis looked the stranger over again waiting for some kind of introduction.

"Why do you look like this?" Curtis asked Jophiel, referring to his appearance.

"Do you mean like a human and not like an angel?"

"Well yes, and like Jesus with the robes and sandals."

"Because this is how we dressed in 2500 B.C. and I felt nostalgic."

Okay, Curtis thought, *I didn't know angels got nostalgic about things. I suppose they are intelligent and feeling super-beings; why wouldn't they get sentimental for better times?*

He looked the stranger over again and felt a little unsettled.

Curtis couldn't take it anymore; he looked directly at the man. "And you are?"

"I am Uriel, the Archangel of the Sun," the stranger said.

"Hello Uriel, Archangel of the Sun. I am Curtis, proprietor of this dream."

"I know who you are, priest."

Priest? The thought of it made Curtis's stomach turn.

It had been over twenty years since Curtis was an altar boy at St. Michael's Church back in his hometown. And even after all this time, the mere suggestion that he resembled anything like the perverted asshole that headed St. Michael's itched at Curtis under his skin. He had completely dropped the Church out of his life, much to the dismay of his staunch Catholic parents. And he even went through a phase where he hated all religion as a whole. But unlike his altar boy brethren, most of whom dropped out of school and became drug dealers or small-time thieves, Curtis stayed out of trouble (for the most part), finished high school, then college and then finally joined the military.

His friend, Derrick, on the other hand, wasn't so lucky. Derrick was Father Sullivan's favourite altar boy. He had even bought Derrick a Timex watch for Christmas, back when Curtis was thirteen years old. At first, Curtis felt the stings of jealously when Derrick opened his present in front of him.

After all, why did Derrick get a gift and he didn't? He served mass just as many times — if not more — than Derrick.

Within the next year, Curtis grew four inches and added fifteen pounds to his skinny frame. That year he also received more attention from Father Sullivan. He went from, "Good job, Curtis!" with a pat on the head, to "Great job, Curtis!" with a pat on the bottom. Initially, Curtis didn't put much thought into it; Father Sullivan was a priest, a holy man. Surely the affection was based on camaraderie, like the slaps that baseball and football players would give each other out on the field. Then the priest's hands began lingering for a second or two after each pat. Curtis could still remember the day, even the exact moment, when Father Sullivan's hand nonchalantly brushed across the front of Curtis and the instinctive tingle that something *wrong* had just occurred. Later that day, Derrick approached Curtis in the playground.

"Hey Derrick, I haven't seen you around for a while. You guys move or something?"

"Um, no, we just went on a kind of *vacation*," Derrick said hesitantly. "Curtis, um... Steve and Johnny were mentioning how close Father Sullivan is getting to you."

Curtis's face turned red. "Ya, so?"

Derrick looked down and played with his fingers, gesturing as if he had something under his nails.

"Has he, you know, rubbed... rubbed you, touched... you, you know, up front?"

Curtis couldn't believe what Derrick had asked him. Right here in the schoolyard, Derrick just asked if Father Sullivan — our priest — felt him up. He wanted to call Derrick an 'effing' jerk, and an idiot, and an asshole. But he didn't; instead, his face burned redder, and hot tears swelled up in his eyes.

"He did it to me too, Curtis," Derrick confessed with his head still low, kicking a patch of grass, "and Steve, and Johnny and Jimmy. He has probably been doing it for years. And rubbing is only the beginning," Derrick's voice cracked.

Curtis had never forgotten about sobbing right there in the schoolyard next to the soccer posts that day. The only saving grace was that those posts happened to be at the far side of the yard. He had never mentioned his talk with Derrick or about Father Sullivan to anyone. Two years later, Derrick's Dodge hit a pole on a back road; he died instantly. Curtis, Steven, John and Jimmy stood together at the back of the church for his funeral. They never opened up about their common affliction at St. Michael's, nor did anyone mention that Derrick's "accident" was his way of dealing with the shame. At seventeen, Derrick misunderstood the shame; it wasn't his shame he was carrying, but the priest's. It took Curtis many years to realize that, and it took him many more still to dissolve the hardened attitude that he had built up as a safeguard. He'd had it for so long that he had forgotten that it was there. It was Vivica that had brought him out of it. But by this time Curtis had already closed his life to the Church.

Curtis turned his attention back to Jophiel.

"So did you visit me in my dream to show me this place?"

"Yes, and now that you have talked with Eavery again, I am sure you have more questions. Plus it's easier to visit in your dreams. Human divinity is at its peak when the subconscious is in control, and the dreams are the most efficient way for angels and humans to meet."

That made Curtis think; he exclaimed, "That's why all the profits and saints had their visions while asleep! I got it, and that's why this dream here is uber vivid — because of you. I can even smell the wild flowers in the air."

"That's correct," Jophiel replied as he looked around at his creation.

"Do angels dream?" Curtis thought aloud.

"Of course we dream — all creatures dream. Even dogs dream. Do you think angels are less than dogs?"

Curtis took a step back; he wasn't sure if Jophiel was

actually hurt by his question or if he was just toying with him.

"No, no that's not what I was getting at," Curtis stammered. "It is just that earth creatures have brains made from matter, with neurons snapping and ions bouncing around creating images. If angels aren't made of the same matter, I didn't know if angels could..."

"Yes, we dream. Curtis you have to stop thinking of everything in existence functioning and reacting like you do." Jophiel turned and started to walk down along the river bank. He reached down and grabbed a stone at the edge of the water and rolled it in his fingers.

"The physics that surrounds *you* is not the only physics that was created. When you use your mind and think about something, you are using an essence of energy that is not matter related; it is more 'angelic'. When an idea pops into your head, your neurons did not create it. No firing synapses or biological reactions occurred."

Curtis wasn't really a deep thinker. He never bought into the multi-verse (multiple universe theory) or multiple dimensions (like Superman's Bizzaro World). This was a totally foreign concept of the world he knew.

"Okay, then where do they come from: *my* ideas?"

"Perhaps from someone else. Maybe from some other time or from some other galaxy."

Curtis stopped walking and looked at Jophiel. "WHAT?"

Is he kidding me? Did he just say from some other galaxy? This dream just moved from the interesting to the stupid.

"Curtis, start thinking of EVERYTHING in the sense of energy. And energy never dies, but changes; it causes things to react and then it moves on." Jophiel walked over and pinched Curtis on the shoulder.

"Ouch!"

"The cells that make up our body are held together by

small atomic charges, almost like your own gravity. These small charges are produced by billions of atoms. We can carry this structural breakdown from the atoms to protons to quarks to gluons, and so forth. When you get hurt and you scream out in pain *like a small girl…*"

"What do you mean – small girl? That pinch was hard," Curtis interrupted defending his pride.

"… that raw emotion is broadcasted off of you. That transmission is affecting everything on your planet, it affects things in the Angel realm and in a few millennia it will affect some other life form in some distant galaxy. So your cry of pain, or your road rage or your intense love making is affecting people you have never met. It is affecting butterflies migrating in Mexico, and it can even affect the oceans."

Curtis rubbed the sore spot; he was finding this philosophy out of his comfort zone. He found it was difficult to grasp — not just with his head, but also with his ego. This goes way beyond New Age — something that Curtis was raised to scoff at and ridicule. But, since these concepts were coming from an angel and not some old lady at a psychic fair reading tea leaves, Curtis opened up and accepted that there might be some truth to it.

"I can understand how the sound of my scream might reach the guy next to me when I am stuck in traffic, but how can my anger affect some kid in the rain forest in Chile?"

Jophiel rolled the stone in his hand again and tossed it into the river. "Just like that stone; do you see the cascading ripples that were created from it? The effect of that stone reaches well beyond the physical limits of the stone itself. The waves will eventually be absorbed by the water causing a billion reactions in the river that you will never see. It is all about energy. Therefore, your anger, caused by the person driving in front of you, is radiating from you. That radiation, when it reaches the subconscious of another person — 'that kid in the rainforest' — is transformed into an idea. Your broadcasted energy, filtered through another person's psyche, creates something new in that person."

Curtis watched the stone's impact in the river gradually disappear.

"So all of our emotions and feelings are constantly being transmitted out of us? And each of us reacts to that everywhere in the world? That sounds very Buddha. I find it hard to believe and even harder to understand. I mean, I haven't had a few billion years to wrap my head around it like you have. Besides," Curtis kicked a stone into the water, creating another series of ripples, "the radio station blasts out megawatts of energy and two hours down the road I lose the signal. I mean..."

"Priest," Uriel interrupted annoyed at the human. "That has to do with the sensitivity of your equipment and its shoddy made on Monday or Friday workmanship. Believe me, the Creator does not make shoddy equipment."

"The mob effect is another example," Jophiel continued. "When a group of people — who individually would not plunder and loot or turn over carriages and carts — gets together, a negative energy rooted deep within them begins to bounce off of them, stimulating each of them so that the negative energy begins to magnify. Ordinarily nice humans can become rioters or murderers just from a simple shift of negative energy. Similarly, some people become overwhelmed from positive energy as it gets magnified at large events, like a church or coven gathering."

Taking in a deep breath, Curtis rubbed his fingers through his hair. He felt the warm sun on his face and heard the sound of the waves lapping up on shore, and for a moment he actually believed he was standing in Israel and not just dreaming it. Then he looked over at Uriel with a bewildered look on his face.

"Uriel, why do you keep calling me priest?"

"You are a priest; I know you well Curtis," Uriel replied.

"I think you are confusing me with some other Curtis Papp. I'm just a corporal in the Royal Canadian Air Force."

Uriel shifted and squared himself with Curtis. "You are a priest. In your eleventh year, you were given Holy Orders. I know this because I am the angel who gave them to you."

As the Archangel spoke, Curtis could feel himself go back to when he was eleven years old.

Uriel's voice divided into six distinct voices then harmonized back into one, drawing Curtis deeper into his past. "You were sleeping in the night when Sagittarius was peeking. I bent over and whispered your name and declared that you have been anointed as a deliverer of His words."

Curtis swayed on his feet, drugged by Uriel's voice. A scene of the event was played out before him— a young Curtis in his old bedroom deep asleep, the impressive figure of the Archangel with his wings folded back, leaning over him whispering into his ear. Curtis was having a dream within a dream.

"Once someone has been anointed with Holy Orders Curtis, they are declared a priest within the heavens," Jophiel added.

The angels were right. Deep down inside Curtis knew he should have gone to a seminary and fulfilled a very strong desire to preach.

But that also brought back buried memories of Father Sullivan and the years in which he was an altar boy.

Uriel, unconcerned about violating privacy, read Curtis's thoughts. "What that man did to you and the other boys scarred you. He changed you enough to alter your destiny. But once you have been given Holy Orders, you are a priest... practicing or not."

"He may have been clothed like a priest, Curtis, but I can assure you that he is not being treated like one in the afterlife," Jophiel revealed.

"Wow, this is a lot to process."

Jophiel laughed aloud. "Sorry, sometimes I get carried away. Is there anything else you would like to know before I return you back?"

Curtis tried to clear his head. Having conversations with ancient divine beings doesn't happen every day. *Although*, Curtis thought, *I guess it happens a lot more now than it used too.*

"Earlier, you mentioned that dreams are the most efficient way to talk to humans. Does that mean angels need food or sustenance of some kind? Do you eat?" Curtis asked the question, but as soon as he heard it aloud he felt stupid for it.

"Yes, of course. But, no, we do not eat Angel Food cake, although, I have heard it is very tasty."

Curtis wasn't sure if he should laugh or not. Jophiel usually spoke in the tone of someone giving directions.

"Okay," Jophiel continued, "We get our *nourishment* from light and cosmic energy. Although gamma rays, x-rays and invisible light energy can affect you by causing DNA damage or sunburns, they feed us. After the Big Bang when God said, 'Let there be light!' He created his first beings — *us* — and we feed off of the divine aura of that first light. Later, He created atoms and particles, which led to matter. And then He created you."

Uriel added, "We are that of energy and light. Some are angels of the full moon, and some are angels of Mars or Jupiter or Saturn. We exist because light and energy exists,"

"What about Demons? What do they eat?"

The angel's moods changed at the thought. "Well, demons *are* angels, but they feed on distorted, tainted energy, which is energy that is filtered through matter." Jophiel could tell Curtis didn't quite understand his last comment.

"Divine light is a pure light; it is pure energy. But when an energy wave travels through matter, the atoms either take away or add to that pulse of energy, changing it, distorting it. And energy taken from matter is the dirtiest of all."

"What about nuclear energy? Does this affect you?"

Jophiel tilted his head and looked at Curtis. "The radiation that is released from it is a literal buffet for all corrupted spirits and demons."

"And the atomic blasts from decades ago and, more recently, your particle colliders emit photons and x-rays which ignited a germination of new beings. Never before in the Universe has a creature of God created energy. It is fowl and unclean," Uriel said as the volume of his voice increased.

"And it is creating beings that should not exist and resurrecting beings that should stay gone." Jophiel, too, was getting excited.

"What do you mean, 'who should not exist?'"

"Demons, priest." Uriel barked.

Jophiel sensed Uriel was losing his patience. Since the destruction of the ancient Nephilim civilizations, Uriel had grown colder and more belligerent toward humans. He thought bringing Uriel back with him to better times might have loosened his heart a little toward humans, but perhaps it might have just added salt to the wound.

"Humans have taken what is rightfully His and, in true human fashion, distorted it and made it your own. You have now created a device that mimics the very moment of creation. But you are not divine and your reasons for knowledge are selfish; therefore, the very energy you create with your machine is instantly tainted. Every time the colliders analyze that divine moment, the energy emitted infects angels like a virus, or strengthens demons, or creates a whole new demon altogether, filling the coffers for Hades," Uriel explained.

Curtis was shocked by what he was hearing. He always liked nuclear energy it always seemed so modern, so green.

Our benign neutral science is directly affecting the balance of Heaven and Hell. That would make a good book.

"Can't God simply blink and wipe out any of the unfortunate things that we have created?"

Uriel exhaled loudly. "You mean like pollution, torture, rape, environmental destruction, the extinction of animals...? The universe exists, and how it exists is because after He set the laws in motion He does not interfere with them."

Curtis was feeling bombarded by this information, which made him feel as though he alone was destroying the world. "Sure He can; He creates miracles all the time."

"No, He doesn't," Jophiel replied softly, trying to relax the conversation. "What people call miracles are their own personal interpretations of a very unlikely event that just happened to work out in their favour. Someone being *miraculously* cured of cancer has the same statistical advantage of someone winning the lottery, and yet every day hundreds of people win the lottery and hundreds of others are cured of cancer. At least they both thank the same person. Yahweh has never altered the laws, and He never will."

Jophiel could tell that Curtis was feeling backed into a corner. He smiled and held his hands up to the sky.

"It is such a beautiful day, let us walk and enjoy it."

Thankful for the topic change, Curtis looked around again and stepped to the edge of the shoreline. He could feel the waves splashing over his open toes. He then noticed for the first time that he too was wearing sandals and was dressed in the ancient garb.

"Can you teach me to walk on water?"

Jophiel shook his head. *What a human!* "Like Jesus? When I am done with you, you won't have to. But sure..."

"Speaking of Jesus," Uriel interjected, "he said something once that was entirely misquoted. Remember when he said he was the..."

CHAPTER SEVENTEEN

Lord Nelson Hotel, Halifax

Lukács always liked the feel of the Audi, the s4 edition in particular. He was glad when the *Társadalom* (Society) finally started switching their international fleet from Mercedes Benz to the more modern luxury style of the Audi, especially for his contracts in North America where his time on the road could be measured in days.

Pulling into the arced driveway of the iconic hotel, Lukács put the Audi in park and handed the valet an American twenty dollar bill from his bill clip. The bellboy, Bill, briskly fetched his luggage from his car and followed him into the main lobby. As he walked through the glass doors, he was greeted by a large gleaming crystal chandelier. It hung suspended ten feet in the air, threatening a small glass table holding a bouquet of roses that was centered directly below it. The highly polished marble floors reflected the turn of the century embossed ceiling. Lukács panned the room, instinctively noting his new surroundings. A second level mezzanine was accessible by stairs on both sides of the lobby. Along the mezzanine were small, intimate tables adorned with fine cloth, and centered on each was a single bloomed carnation within a Swarovski crystal vase. A husband and wife, in their mid-sixties were in a casual conversation. The man was wearing a pearl collared shirt with a silver silk tie and the woman wore a deep purple and black dress that seemed to blend and alternate the colours as she shifted in her seat. She cupped the large glass of red wine in her hands and Lukács noticed she was wearing a very large diamond ring on a white gold band; it struck him as gaudy costume jewelry, but he was quite certain it was an authentic diamond.

The foyer's six pillars were encased in richly stained red oak that ran throughout the room as a continual garnish for the gleaming brass and marble interior. In direct contrast to the room's elegant and regal impression, a flat screen T.V. was mounted on the center pillar; it displayed the city's transit schedules, dinner theatre and local sports timings.

"Right this way, sir," Bill said as he scurried to the dark marbled reception desk. A large nineteenth-century painting of a flotilla of tall ships in some elusive harbor was mounted behind the attendant.

"Good afternoon sir," smiled the twenty-something receptionist. "Can I help you?"

Lukács instantly categorized the woman. She had a short, bob-styled hair cut, and was wearing a smart charcoal-black suit. Her polished brass nametag spelled *Louise* in calligraphy.

"Macdonald, Stephen."

The young professional quickly typed his name into her computer. If she was surprised by his accented English, her welcoming smile didn't reveal it. Configuring an electronic key card, she placed it in a small folder and set it in front of him.

"Your room is 414," she said and handed him a pen. "Please sign here."

As Lukács penned his new alias onto the reservation contract, Louise continued with her hostess orientation.

"If you desire, our Victory Arms restaurant will be serving authentic English pub fare until 11 p.m. Enjoy your visit to our wonderful ..."

At that point, Lukács's attention focused on getting into his room and all he heard was *blah blah blah.*

"Thank you," he replied, not caring if she was finished with her speech or not.

As he walked into his hotel room, the bellboy placed his suitcase on the bench at the foot of his queen-sized bed and his leather laptop case on the desk.

"We have wireless internet for your convenience, Mr. MacDonald," the bellboy interjected, trying to create small talk.

"Yes, I know," Lukács said making it clear he wasn't interested in talking.

Another son-of-a-bitchin hotel room, in another son-of-a-bitchin city, with another son-of-a-bitchin bellboy chatting me over and trying to butter me up for a tip. Bill probably isn't his real name.

The young man walked over to the opened door. Turning smartly and with a large smile he looked over at the man.

"Is there anything else I can get for you, Mr. MacDonald?"

Maybe a joint to help loosen you up, you uptight bastard? Bill thought to himself.

Lukács walked over to Bill, pulled out a ten and handed it to him. "No," he said, lifting the door stop with his foot allowing the door to close in the bellboy's face.

"Thank you," was all Bill could get out before the door securely shut.

"Oh, I hope he orders from room service tonight," the bellboy mumbled to himself.

Lukács walked over to the window and looked down at the city and at the Public Gardens directly across the street.

The Public Gardens were opened in 1867 for the city's more prominent citizenry to sip tea in its Victorian-style gardens. Today, its two acres are secured behind black wrought iron fencing, and an antique iron gate: a virtual time bubble surrounded by the hectic urban setting of modern Halifax.

He watched as people strode through the Gardens. Some were feeding the ducks and geese at the pond while others took their daily walks along the paths. A few others sat on folding chairs at the large gazebo, listening to a military band play Heart of Oak.

Turning back to his room, Lukács unzipped his leather case and pulled out his laptop. After accessing the WiFi network, he logged onto the *Angyal Paranesfájl*, the KRÁJCÁR secured website used for keeping in touch with Veszprém and updating orders.

It also has the Ascension Locator, which is specialized software that locates the KRÁJCÁR holy site and indicates in which direction to pray from any location on the planet.

The *Testvériség* (Brotherhood) has a strict code for prayers for its members. They require its priests and counsel to pray towards the Ascension site, the Zala River, near what had become (in the eyes of the KRÁJCÁR) the holy city of Zalaegerszeg in the heart of Hungary.

It is well-known within the KRÁJCÁR, that the Prophet Attila was poisoned during his wedding ceremony and died later that night of internal bleeding. Later, his men temporarily redirected the Zala River and buried Attila within three coffins (one gold, one silver and one iron) under the riverbed. They then returned the river to hide the exact burial site. The funeral celebration lasted for three days in which Attila, like many prophets throughout history, ascended to heaven as a whole person on that last day; he sits among his brothers at the right hand of Yahweh.

Opening his suitcase, Lukács pulled out his prayer rug

and compass. Finding his bearing, he laid out his mat on the floor. He lit two white candles and positioned one north and the other south. He then went down on both knees and prostrated towards the holy site. Prayer wasn't necessary until dawn, but a new room required cleansing and it helped Lukács clear his mind.

The *Testvériség* had fifteen prayers altogether, but five canon prayers that must be recited every day: The Ascension Prayer, the Prophet's Decree, the Loyalty Prayer, the Words of Strength and the Prayer for Peace and Blessing of Mind. Lukács knew them all by heart. His mother prepared him from childhood to become a sanctified brother within the KRÁJCÁR. She forced him as a little boy to pray all fifteen prayers every day before school.

School was something that came easy to Lukács. He was always good at mathematics and the sciences. One time in his second year of high school he wrote the medical sciences entrance exam for the Semmelweis University in Budapest. He didn't know why he wrote it because he knew his mother would never let him attend. Perhaps a desire to be normal momentarily surfaced in his subconscious. Months went by and he forgot all about it until, one day after school, he walked into the kitchen and saw an opened letter from the university sitting on the table. He felt his heart sink in his chest.

Swallowing hard, he leaned over the table. With his hands trembling, he decided to read it while it rested against the marmalade jar.

With no previous medical studies and still in middle high school he aced the exam with a ninety-three percent. The university was dispatching a recruiter to his home address to discuss financial grants and loans and immediate acceptance once he graduates.

For a short moment, Lukács felt proud of himself; perhaps there was a normal life out there waiting for him.

"Lukács, come in here," his mother called from the other room.

She sat in her rocking chair, facing the window. Her prayer beads were coiled in her fingers. Lukács's throat dried and his chest tightened as he looked at his *Anya*.

"Igen Anya?" barely escaped his lips. His eyes watched her as her mouth silently muttered her prayers, her fingers graduating through the chain of beads as she finished one prayer and moved to the next.

The only light in the small room came from the window, creating a dim and unwelcoming atmosphere. She let him stand there in the doorway watch her while she prayed, while she rocked, and while her fingers moved from bead to bead to bead.

It will give him time to think about his sins.

And it did. Lukács knew he never should have written that test. *What was I thinking? I knew it was wrong. Why did I do it?* The questions floated through his mind. Long gone was the feeling of pride and desire for normalcy. Now shame and guilt filled his stomach, bile rising in his throat. *How could I have been so selfish?*

Lukács's family had always been part of the Testvériség. His mother had preached his destiny his entire life, and this was a slap in her face.

As he watched her rock back and forth, he noticed her wooden cane leaning against the window sill. She never used it for walking; it only came out for discipline. Oh, he knew that cane well. It had put him in the hospital for three days during his freshman year.

One time a girl new to his school made nice with him one day in math class. So at lunch he started tutoring her and after school he would walk her home even though it was the wrong direction and added six kilometers to his own walk. Lukács was happy. He was very happy. She made all the other crap in his life seem bearable. He was falling in love for the first time.

Then his mother found a note she had written him. He didn't know how she found it. He was sure he kept this letter, like all her letters, in a box under a pile of wood behind the shed. But she found it. Maybe while going through his dresser drawers, or snooping under his bed or between the mattresses like she always did.

"What is this?" she said as she threw the love letter in his face.

He was stunned and didn't know what to say, what to do. But he knew it was going to hurt.

"I have told you and told you Lukács, but you do not listen. Maybe Ha-Sata whispers in your ear and makes you stupid like your father."

Lukács wasn't sure; he didn't remember his father.

"Girls are a nuisance. They are a distraction. You must first become a *Brother* before you defile yourself with these... these whores," she lectured.

"This 'Niki,' I know of her. She is not a true Magyar. Her grandmother is a *Roma*," she said in disgust and he watched her spit on the freshly polished floor.

"I will not have a son of mine seeding a child with a dirty *Roma*." Again she spit on the floor.

Lukács knew his mother had no idea who Niki was or even her grandmother for that matter, but there was no talking to her when she was in her rage.

He opened his mouth to say he was sorry, to *say nothing sexual ever happened* and that she would like Niki if she gave her a chance. But he never got the chance to. The very moment his lips parted, the room shook and violently tumbled; excruciating pain erupted in his jaw and blood flooded his mouth. It took him five or six seconds to realize his mother had just struck him in the face with her cane. As much as that first strike hurt, the next one hurt even more.

The third strike broke his jaw. He couldn't tell how many he received altogether, but the hospital and follow-up police reports mentioned something about falling thirty steps down into the basement, which of course was false. After three quiet, drug-filled days in the hospital, his mother signed him out, no questions asked.

Yes Lukács knew that cane well.

"...Holy Attila, Amen," his mother said under her breath as she finished her prayers.

She gently untwined her prayer beads and placed them in their jeweled carrying box. Standing up in front of the window she looked out at the traffic passing by. Shaking her head she tried to understand where she went wrong. Why her son would disrespect her like this.

Ha-Sata is tempting him again, trying to divert his attention, his will, away from his destiny, away from God's work and away from the Prophet's work. There is only one way to remove Ha-Sata's hold on my beloved Lukács.

His mother reached over and grabbed her cane. Her hands were shaking; she didn't like to hit her Lukács. She hated it. But Ha-Sata, the Tempter, the Satan, will not take her son from her like he did his father.

She turned and looked at the young man standing in the doorway. She could see the fear in his eyes. Without saying a word, Ha-Sata's grip was already failing her prodigy. Unfortunately, it will take a lot more than just a look to completely exorcize this demon.

"My beautiful Lukács, your whole life you have been plagued by Ha-Sata and his demons. And every time I have been there to protect your immortal soul. The Prophet Attila has called me by name; he has told me to *finally* defeat the Satan that holds you so dearly."

It was obvious to Lukács that he was in for another beating, but her emphasis on 'finally' struck fear deep into him.

I need to run. Run and leave this twisted place.

But he didn't. He stood there in the doorway as his mother approached him with her cane. Somewhere deep inside him he believed his mother was protecting him. He believed he was a special child, and his destiny was not her delusion, but an actual calling from the Prophet. Somehow he knew this would be the last time his beloved and tortured Anya would ever need to take out that cane.

Calmness washed over Lukács. He stepped into the dimly lit room knowing that he would never see it again.

In the hotel room, Lukács thought back to that moment like he had thousands of times before. He could still remember the exact moment when Satan's authority over his soul was released forever. He didn't know how many hits it took; there were far too many to count. Ha-Sata's grasp was strong and determined, but not as determined as his saintly Anya.

Even today he can remember, as his life began to leave his broken body, his mother kneeling beside him kissing his forehead, crying and reciting the Prophet's Decree. After several months in the Intensive Care Unit and almost one full year at the Veszprém hospital, Lukács went to live with his uncle Elek and his cousin Khagan. He had never seen his sweet Anya again.

But every day during his daily prayers, he hears his mother's voice reciting the Prophet's Decree, sounding exactly like she did the day she saved his soul.

When Lukács finished his prayers, he rolled up the prayer rug and blew out the candles. He flipping through the folder and studied his next assignment.

This guy was older than usual — in his thirties and with a family. He noticed that the number of assignments have increased within the last twelve months, which means there are more of them *changing*.

"Ha-Sata is preparing something," he said aloud to himself.

"And these abominations are having children. They too will have to been taken care of."

He didn't particularly enjoy killing children. It was an unfortunate necessity he did without question. It was inconceivable to doubt the orders of the Testvériség and the Holy Társadalom. God's work may seem harsh to us on earth but His plan will be revealed to us in time and our loyalty will guarantee a place in paradise.

Flipping through the pages he realized something: *This fucker has a weekend routine.*

CHAPTER EIGHTEEN

Dalhousie University, Halifax

Curtis walked up the grey granite steps of the Life Sciences Center. Walking down the large hall with its very high ceiling, Curtis could hear his footsteps echoing off the stone walls and stair cases. As he traversed the corridors he could hear Vivica giving her lecture in the auditorium of the Department of Earth Sciences. The reverberation of her voice off the granite and marble hallways gave it an eerie sound, like someone trying to communicate from the "other side."

As Curtis approached the lecture hall, the center wooden door was propped open. In classic Roman amphitheatre style, chairs with a foldaway desktop faced the lecture stage.

Vivica was going over the final preparations of the trip to Ireland with twenty-one of her geology students.

"So most of us will be flying out of Halifax on Saturday at 9 a.m., try to show up at the airport at least an hour and a half early. Josh? You said you and Brad and Chris are heading out tonight?"

"Yes, Mrs. Papp."

"Good!" she said checking them off the list in front of her.

"And Jasmine and Faith, you girls are flying out on the first flight Sunday morning? Jasmine? Hello?"

Looking up from her roster, Vivica watched the young nineteen year old texting on her phone. "Jasmine, could you please put the iPhone down for one second? Thank you."

The crowd laughed as the girl meekly slipped her phone into her purse. "Sorry!"

"It's all right, but you and Faith *are* ready to go for Sunday?"

"Yes, Mrs. Papp."

"Great. Now this excursion is a big deal. This is costing you and the university a lot of money, so let's make the best use of our time there. We have two weeks, which isn't a lot of time to study 40,000 stone columns of the Giant's Causeway. I will be staying at the Bushmills Inn on Dunluce Road, right inside the town of Bushmills. I believe all of you have decided to stay at the Youth Hostel Associate, also right in Bushmills. Good, so now I can keep an eye on you more easily.

If no one has any questions, I will see most of you at the airport and the rest of you in Ireland. *Slán a fhágáilag duine. Goodbye.*"

As the herd of teenagers stampeded up the stairs, Curtis ducked into one of the isles to prevent himself from being trampled. Under his breath he *mooed* and *grunted.*

Organizing her itinerary, Vivica looked up and saw her husband walking down the steps.

"You are just in time; I just finished," she said smiling.

"I noticed. I was almost killed up there. Those teenagers," his voice fluttered, "those teenagers are sooo dangerous," he said with an over-acting flare.

"You are such a boob!" Vivica shook her head, laughing.

"Thank you! It just so happens, I like boobs."

"Tell me about it! I think I am still bruised from last time," she said as she readjusted herself under her bra.

"Oh, sorry about that!"

"So what do I owe for the great honour of your visit?" she asked.

"Well, Sarge let me off early, so I thought I would pick up some really good, really expensive wine for tonight — you know, before you fly out tomorrow morning and leave me alone for two weeks," Curtis winked at her. "And I can only find the good stuff downtown," he explained. "And I thought maybe we could go for a coffee before we pick Charlie up at daycare."

"Mmmm, a coffee sounds pretty good," she said as she stepped down from the stage.

"Wine, eh?" she looked sideways at him.

"Yeah! Really good wine," he replied playfully. "And a movie. I was thinking one of the really *good* movies."

"You mean the kind of movies that we watch when Charlie is gone to bed?"

Curtis wasn't sure if that was a question or a statement.

"Sounds good to me," Vivica replied.

"That was easy," Curtis chuckled.

"Yep, and you better have them add a few shots of espresso to your coffee. I think you're going to need it," she said teasingly and then strutted up the stairs ahead of him.

Halifax Stanfield International Airport

Early the next morning Charlie reached up and kissed her mother goodbye.

"Have a good trip studying rocks, mommy," Charlie said, giving her mother her bravest smile.

"I sure will and I will even bring a piece back for you. Would you like that?"

Charlie's big blue eyes sparkled. "Yes."

"What about me?" Curtis said smirking. "What are you going to bring me back? Haggis?"

"Curtis, Haggis is Scottish. I'll bring you back some authentic Guinness... straight from the Duty Free Shop."

"I'll take it," Curtis said laughing.

A cab honked to let them know they were illegally taking up his reserved parking spot.

"Okay, okay!" Curtis said, waving. "Charlie we have to get going."

"You be sure to take care of your dad while I am gone."

"I will mommy," the four year old replied, her smile beginning wane.

Vivica looked over at Curtis. "And Curtis, stay off *those* websites."

Busted, Curtis shrugged his shoulders. "Hey two weeks is a *looong* time."

Vivica laughed and shook her head. Charlie started to cry as she climbed back into the car.

"It's okay, Peanut; she'll be back before you know it."

Vivica gave them each a kiss and a final "I love you," and headed into the airport.

From the airport, Curtis took Charlie over to the Alderney Landing Farmer's Market in Dartmouth which is where they go every Saturday morning during the summer months. After collecting his weekly supply of fresh produce and occasional spicy Samosa from the Indian woman, they walk through the aisles where vendors sell everything from hand-made pretzels and home-made soaps to beach glass jewelry and organic honey.

Passing MacAskill's Restaurant they walked out the side entrance to a small public park. The playground was built in the shape of a boat and every Saturday Charlie plays with the other Saturday farmer's market kids. Walking out onto the interlocking brick promenade, Curtis watched as the two masts of a small boat tied to the jetty rocked back and forth.

On the Halifax side, two Carnival Cruise ships were docked over by Pier 21.

The low rain clouds prevented Curtis from seeing Elohim City directly. Instead, an ominous golden glow flickered and filtered through the clouds.

It began to rain as Curtis and Charlie stepped outside.

"Oh, daddy, it's raining," Charlie whined.

"Sorry, Charlie, I don't think we should go to the playground; it will be too slippery and dangerous. I don't want you to hurt yourself."

"I guess not," Charlie pouted.

"Come on, I will get you some homemade ice cream," Curtis bribed Charlie before she could turn the pout into a full-fledged scene. It had been too many times that Curtis had to pick Charlie up and carry her out to the car and let Vivica finish the shopping because Charlie wanted something, and when she doesn't get what she wants she lets the world know she is dissatisfied.

Curtis started to turn around when he noticed Brent, one of the guys from Lin's Vietnamese restaurant. He was sitting on the edge of the bench dressed in running shorts and a t-shirt. He was staring at a large propeller mounted to a cement podium that once belonged to the Canadian Coast Guard Ship the *John A. MacDonald*. Occasionally, Brent would blink or move his lips, saying something inaudible.

"Look at that man, daddy," Charlie pointed. "He's getting wet."

"Yes he is," Curtis said concerned. "You wait right here under the canopy; I am going to say hi to him, okay?"

"Sounds good to me; I don't to want get wet," Charlie said candidly.

Curtis did a double-take. The things she said sometimes made him wonder if there was an old soul in that young body.

Brent raised his hand and began caressing the air as if he

was petting an invisible dog. As Curtis got closer he noticed the blank stare in Brent's eyes. *Is he having a seizure or maybe tripping out on some kind of drug?*

The rain started to come down heavier and Curtis observed that it had no affect on Brent. He looked back at Charlie. *At least she's dry.*

He watched people in the window pointing at Brent and laughing. He felt embarrassed, not only for Brent but also for himself — for knowing Brent.

"Hey, Brent!" Curtis called out.

Brent just continued to pet his invisible dog.

"Hey pal, what are you doing all by yourself? You better get along with the others," Brent mumbled.

Curtis frowned. "What? Brent what did you just say? Come on, man, it's raining and you and *I* are getting soaked. Let's get to my car; I'll drive you home."

Brent still didn't move, but at least he stopped petting the air. Curtis reached over and put his hand on Brent's shoulder.

"Brent!" Curtis said. His voice sounded hollow and reverberated like he was speaking into a large metal cauldron.

The park and harbor quickly pixilated away and Curtis was standing next to Brent in a rocky expanse of a rolling pasture. One lone sheep was slowly trotting back to a large herd grazing on the rich clover.

Startled, Brent fell over on to the ground.

"Curtis? What are you doing here?"

"I... I don't know," Curtis stumbled. "What is this place?"

"I think I'm having a *remembering*. Are you real?" Brent stood and examined Curtis. "I have never had a conversation with someone during a *remembering* before."

He raised his hand and poked Curtis in the shoulder, half expecting his hand to float through him.

"How did you get in here?" Brent asked, still amazed.

Curtis had to focus. He was shocked to be there too.

"I'm not sure. We saw you sitting on the bench getting soaked in the rain, so I came over to get you. When I touched you, I showed up here."

"No way!" Brent exclaimed excitedly. "So you can 'warp' into another person's *rememberings*? That's fucking weird."

Curtis couldn't believe it himself. "Yeah, that is fucking weird."

He looked around. The deep green fields, the blue sky — it was a complete contrast to the weather back in Halifax. Thinking of Halifax reminded him of Charlie.

"I have to get back. My four year old daughter is standing by herself back in the real world. You have to snap out of this." Curtis heard the stress rising in his own voice.

"I don't know how to, Curtis. This is like my third time. It does what it wants. I can't control it," Brent said, also beginning to feel trapped.

Not good enough, Curtis thought as panic started to tighten his chest.

"End this NOW!" Curtis yelled staring at Brent, his voice booming through the cloudless sky.

Immediately, both men were back standing in front of the bench, drenched from the rain. Brent blinked in surprise to be back. He folded his arms in front of his chest, aware for the first time that he was wet and cold.

Curtis quickly looked back at the building for Charlie. She wasn't there — *oh my God where is* —

"Daddy! Daddy! Daddy!"

Curtis looked down at Charlie tugging on his fingers. Curtis took a deep breath, trying to relax the tension that had built up.

"Hey, Peanut, let's get out of the rain," Curtis said looking down at her. "Brent, do you want a ride home?"

"Sure, that would be great. Sorry if I get your car wet," Brent apologized in advance, still a little dazed.

"It'll dry, don't worry about it," Curtis said.

"How did you do that? How did you show up in there?" Brent questioned.

"I don't know. That was the first time."

"How did you snap us out of it?" Brent continued to question.

Curtis shook his head. *Yes, how did I do that?*

They cut back through the market to avoid the rain as much as possible. Curtis caught a few snickers and finger-pointing as they walked through the crowd.

"Get caught in the rain, did ya?" an old man asked, chuckling from behind his table of art-deco drift wood.

"No, me and my daddy was standing next to a man who bit into a Trident Splash gum and we got caught in the wave," Charlie sarcastically replied talking loud enough for everyone around to hear. The group of people near his table broke out laughing.

"You've been told George!" a reply came from the crowd that brought more laughter and attention away Curtis and Brent. The man's smirk fell off his face and he sat back down in his chair.

Curtis messed Charlie's hair and smiled at her. How could a four year old come up with that? Again he got that nagging feeling she was an old soul.

Taking the pedestrian bridge over the train tracks and the escalator down into the Alderney Gate building, they stepped out onto Alderney Drive. The overhang of the building shielded them from the rain.

"I parked just up the street there," Curtis said pointing to his Honda.

"So do you come out to the farmer's market every Saturday?" Curtis asked.

Brent, shivering from the wet and cold, looked over. "No.

Every Saturday morning around nine, I go for my 7 km jog. It's really the only time I get to myself. My wife, Janice, works evening all week and our son, Bruce, consumes our spare time."

"I know what you mean," Curtis replied flashing Charlie a smile and squeezed her hand.

"It looks like the rain is stopping, daddy."

Curtis looked out across the intersection; indeed, the rain was slowing.

"Well, Charlie, let's hurry to the car, maybe you still have a chance of staying somewhat dry."

As they exited out from under the extended roof and approached the road, a speeding white Chevy cube van flew up onto the curb.

In a blink of an eye, the world slowed to an almost stop. The rain drops seemed to be suspended in mid-air, and the traffic passing in both directions looked to be at a virtual standstill. Brent had his left foot suspended over a puddle of water with an almost comical and inevitable conclusion of getting even wetter. But Curtis's heightened sense of danger for himself and Charlie was anything but humorous. The realization that the speeding van was only a few feet away and still tearing towards them caused Curtis to react. Holding onto Charlie's hand, he blindly leaped backwards, pulling his daughter with him. Within the next second, he felt both his feet being struck by the bumper and right headlight of the van, pitching him off into a spin with Charlie firmly grasped within his arms. Curtis landed on his back with a *crack* and tumbled into the brick pillar and metal trash can. Charlie looked up at him, her eyes wide with terror, as she watched Curtis gasp for air.

Brent, however, wasn't so lucky. He received the full impact of the van's bumper and grill. Whatever life he had remaining when he was flung off the sidewalk left him when his skull collided with the steel lamp post.

The van sped down Alderney Drive, side swiping a small silver car that was stopped at the traffic light, steam escaping from under its hood.

Charlie still looking up into her father's face started to cry. "Daddy, daddy, are you okay?"

Curtis tried to answer her; he wanted to assure her that he was all right, but he couldn't get any air into his lungs. And he was pretty sure he had one or two broken ribs. Curtis's ears began to ring as he watched Charlie cry in his arms. *God I hope she wasn't hurt.*

A sonorous ringing in his ears quickly drowned out all other sounds. *Someone... ambulance... accident.*

It was the last thing Curtis heard before the world went black.

A few hours later Curtis woke up in a brightly-lit hospital room.

"Daddy, you're awake," Charlie said, lying beside him and looking up.

The world was not quite in focus yet, but he could still make out the beautiful face of his daughter.

At first, Curtis had forgotten all about being hit by the van, but then a sharp pain in his chest brought it all back.

"How are you, Peanut?" he whispered.

"I'm okay, daddy," Charlie whispered back.

"How are you feeling?" Eavery said from somewhere.

"Like I got hit by a truck," he grunted as he unsuccessfully tried to sit up.

"It was more like a van. The Military Police picked it up in Highfield Park."

Curtis lifted his head off the pillow and saw Eavery leaning on the window sill.

"How is Brent doing?" Curtis asked, still in a daze.

"He didn't make it. He was pronounced *dead* (he mouthed the word) at the scene."

Holy shit! His poor family.

Eavery then leaned in close so Charlie couldn't hear. "They also murdered his wife and their little son, Bruce." Eavery could barely get it out.

Curtis's world stopped. "What? This wasn't a stupid accident?"

"No, Curtis. This was a hit. They knew who he was."

"What about me? Charlie?" Curtis asked, feeling the walls of the room closing in on him.

"No, I don't think so. Not yet anyways. You and Charlie were just in the wrong place at the wrong time. It was a miracle you survived. How did you anyway? "

Curtis thought back to the accident and told Eavery the feeling of danger he experienced and how the world slowed down to a near stop.

"If they know about him, do you think they know about anyone else?" Curtis asked, bringing himself back to the present.

"Probably," Eavery replied. "And he only just changed about a month ago. That means there is someone close by."

Coughing and sitting up higher, Curtis repositioned himself. For the first time he noticed his feet were bandaged up. Charlie started to get off the bed to give him more room.

"No, no Peanut. You can stay right here beside me." Through the intense pain, Curtis pulled her closer to him and wrapped an arm around her.

"Eavery, how did you know we were here?"

"I took the ferry over from the Halifax side. When I got off, I heard some of the sellers at the market talking about a smart remark a little girl just made. And one of my 'abilities' gives me a kind of intuition of events that have recently taken place. It rarely proves beneficial, except for maybe finding lost keys. But, I knew you, Charlie and Brent were nearby, so I went looking for you."

"Now what?" Curtis asked. "We can't go to the police. We are stuck in some ridiculous Stephen King life and death, heaven against hell scenario, with an ancient multinational organization out to assassinate each and every one of us for being angel hybrids," Curtis rambled.

The shock of the recent event was too much for him. Tears started to stream down his face. Charlie reached up with a Kleenex and wiped them.

"Thank you, Peanut," his voice quivered. "What time is it?"

Eavery looked at his watch. "11:55 A.M."

Vivica wouldn't be landing in London until early tomorrow morning and it'll be late evening before she gets to her room in Ireland. At least she will be safe out of the country for a while. That thought brought Curtis some relief.

"So what are we going to do, Eavery?" Curtis asked.

"Well, I suggest you move and change your name."

"That's it? I just keep moving, keep changing my name? That's no way to live," Curtis retorted.

"You're wrong, Curtis — that's how to stay alive," Eavery returned.

"I just can't pick up and leave. I'm in the military. People go to prison for shit like that."

"Then request a posting somewhere and get you and your family relocated to another base. That shouldn't be too difficult."

Right now Curtis would do anything to keep his family safe, but there has to be a better solution than constantly running away. A wave of exhaustion washed over him.

Sitting up and pulling the blankets off, Curtis looked down at his bandaged feet. The tight wrappings around his chest confirmed what he already knew: a few broken ribs.

CHAPTER NINETEEN

Sudbury Neutrino Observatory
(SNO), Sudbury, Ontario

At 2073 meters below the city of Sudbury, deep in the Creighton mine, Jake Rogus leaned back in his chair and tilted it on two legs. He watched the green bands of the bar graph fluctuate up and down along with its corresponding numerical values on his computer screen. The graph displays the neutrino quantity flowing into the chamber.

Neutrinos are neutral elementary particles created by stars from the nuclear fusion and decay of their core. The Earth's sun produces approximately two hundred trillion-trillion particles per second that travel uninhibited through matter (including plants, people and even the Earth itself). The Sudbury Neutrino Observatory is one of the world's deepest scientific laboratories. The *chamber,* or what has become affectionately called the *"Death Star"* is a twelve meter wide, five centimeter thick acrylic tank filled with 1000 tons of *heavy* water known as deuterium, and is surrounded by 9600 photomultiplier tubes. As the neutrino passes through the deuterium, it changes a neutron in the heavy water to a proton, and the neutrino to an electron. This new electron-neutrino emits a flash of light, referred to as Cherenkov Radiation. That flash of light is detected by the photomultiplier tubes.

Over a year ago, Jake graduated with a Master's Degree in Astrophysics from the University of Western Ontario in London. He had every intention of getting his doctorate and applying for a position at the Jet Propulsion Laboratory at the California Institute of Technology in Pasadena until he got a knock on his door one rainy Saturday morning. Danielle Fossier stood on the top step close to the storm door, doing whatever she could to get out of the cold October rain.

Not expecting anyone in particular, especially not Danielle Fossier, Jake took his time answering the door. "If it is another Jehovah Witness, he can stay in the rain a little longer," he said to himself.

When he finally opened the door, he was surprised to see Danielle standing there completely soaked with her make-up dripping off her chin.

The eye shadow and liner streaking down her cheeks reminded Jake of Heath Ledger's portrayal of the Joker in *Batman: The Dark Knight.*

He wasn't sure if he was more surprised that she was standing soaking wet in the rain or just standing on his porch; after all, he didn't know how she knew his address, or even his last name, for that matter.

Cautiously looking around the neighbourhood, he let her into his home. Confused by the visit, he went into the kitchen and grabbed a tea towel so she could dry herself off.

"Danielle?" he said a little unsure. *I think her name is Danielle.* "What can I do for you?"

Accepting the towel, Danielle wiped her face and then ran the towel up and over her the bangs of her hair.

"Jake," Danielle said and began to cry, "I'm pregnant."

Jake stood there, one... two... three seconds before he clued in that she was accusing him of being the father. At first he became defensive.

"What? How do you know it's mine? That was one party during Frosh week." Then he became offensive. "This is bullshit! How dare you show up on my doorstep a month later, and claim this... this..." he waved at her stomach, "this is fucking bullshit. You probably got banged a dozen times that week."

Danielle sobbed even harder.

"I didn't sleep with anyone else," she yelled back at him.

"So, then get an abortion," Jake snarled. He hoped the demand would shatter her little charade.

"No, I will not. I don't believe in them."

"I don't believe this," he said to himself. "Then I want a paternity test."

"Well, they cost twelve hundred dollars," she countered, still crying.

"I'll pay for half of it," Jake spit out. The realization of their conversation slowly trickled into his world.

"Where am I going to find six hundred dollars? I'm a freshman."

"I don't know. Student loans? Ask a friend? Ask your father? Tell him it is added school expenses."

Danielle stood there on the rubber matt, dripping wet, sobbing with her arms at her sides. He reached over and put a hand on her shoulder, going through the motions of someone who cared. A world of confusion and confliction filled Jake's head. His perfectly scheduled life was tumbling out of control. He envisioned in the back of his mind the sunny California sky, the warm Pacific Ocean and the ego-swelling position at the JPL slipping away, and darkness closing in, confining, and smothering. Like falling into a deep well, he could envision far off into the distance the blue sky, imagine the warm, dry earth, hear the birds happily chirp and twitter. But all he could feel was her cold, wet jacket and all he could hear was her crying.

Even months later, he never forgot the irony associated

with how he felt on that early Saturday morning and his new job as data analyst 2073m below the blue sky and singing birds. As to the warm earth, well, down at two thousand meters, the earth is 40°C.

Back in the present as Jake was leaning back in his chair, he looked over at the picture; an aerial view of the Jet Propulsion Laboratory grounds. He daydreamed of the sun, sand and bikinis.

Then, out of the corner of his eye, he spied the dome's pressure readings on the bar graph dip down and changing from green into cautionary orange. The computer automatically released more nitrogen into the chamber to compensate for the pressure drop. The thermal sensors also indicated a change in temperature, dropping 1°C. Back up on the surface, a one degree variation could be caused by a lone cloud floating by; however, this deep in the earth's crust, the slightest temperature change becomes significant.

Jake, still absorbed in self-pity, took the readings and logged the event. Looking over the data, he noticed the last analyst logged three similar events within his shift; each anomaly eventually returned back to an acceptable reading.

"That's funny," Jake said to himself. "Ron never logged any comments about the changes, and never mentioned it during the shift changeover."

Moron.

Standing up and stretching his legs, he gave his back and neck a 180 twist. Grabbing his hard hat, he stepped out of the control room. The air conditioning, used in maintaining the computer and equipment in the control room, also kept the technician comfortable. Immediately, the humidity of the old nickel mine hit Jake solidly.

"Holy shit," he mumbled to himself. "That's why Ron never added any comments; he never left the control room."

Walking down the hallway towards the neutrino chamber, it was easy to forget that this was deep underground. False walls and drop ceiling were built into the shaft to give the scientists a sense of working in an office setting. They even went as far as mounting a scenic photo of Ramsey Lake and the surrounding conservation area into fake windows to add to the illusion, but this only added to Jakes bitterness and longing for California. When Jake arriving at the end of the "hall," he swiped his ID card and punched in the six digit security code. Pushing open the metal door, Jake stepped from the clean vinyl-tiled floor to a rough, steel-grated platform. Standing at the top of a cavern, Jake looked over and around the massive *Death Star.*

The fluorescent lights in the hallway behind him dimmed, flickered, and then went black. The emergency lights running off their battery packs mounted into the walls came to life, giving Jake more of a "deer in the headlights" sensation than one of comfort. When the world goes dark at two kilometers down, it goes black.

Oh great! Not overly concerned because the battery backup should have over a full hour's worth of charge, Jake began walking around the chamber to check the numbers on the gauges.

"This is bullshit!" Jake yelled out loud, hearing his voice echo back between the blown concrete walls and the *Death Star*'s metal and acrylic frame.

A multi-billion, multi-national scientific enterprise like this and we're running off diesel generators and the city's dirty power. Unbelievable! Jake thought to himself.

Straining his eyes to read the gauges, Jake decided to go back to the control room and get his flashlight. He closed the metal door behind him and shielded his eyes from the blinding beam of emergency light blaring down in his direction.

Walking down the hall, Jake watched as the emergency lighting flickered and then too-went out.

Jake was in absolute darkness; He stopped walking. Anger bubbled up inside him.

He hated his job, he hated living in Ontario, and he hated being a father. He hated his fucking life.

"AHHH!" he yelled out with both frustration and annoyance.

He blindly reached over and found the wall. Cautiously he started to walk towards the control room. Jake knew the hallway was clean of any obstacles but he instinctively took small steps. His foot falls sounded hollow on the raised floor. Rage pumped blood through his ears, creating a virtual sound of rushing water. His fingers found the edge of the faux window pane. Calculating he was only about halfway, he exhaled loudly; he thought he had travelled much further down the hallway by now.

His palms slid across the warm glass and he thought of the absurd picture of the lake and surrounding forest.

I quit! That's it, I quit. Today is my last day.

"I quit!" he yelled out into the darkness, his voice falling short in the fabricated room's still air.

Then he heard a rustling noise ahead of him.

Jake stopped cold. *Rats! There are rats in here now? Impossible!*

In order to get down into the complex, Jake, like every person and every piece of equipment, had to go through a clean room. Each person had to shower and change into sterilized work clothes while all of their personal property was re-washed by the underground laundry facility. This was another bone of contention with Jake. Because they worked 2 km underground and the excessiveness of the clean freaks, the technicians and scientists worked on a 21-day shift rotation, staying in individually cramped and sparsely decorated dorm-style living quarters. Add 100% fluorescent lighting and recycled air; Jake was surprised he didn't quit earlier.

There was more rustling. *What is that?*

Jake's brain rapidly tried to identify the sound and match it to possible causes. Perhaps the air conditioners and filters were being upgraded. The observatory maintains a very specific humidity percentage. If the air is too dry then static charges build up in the air, threatening the very sensitive electronic equipment and its data. Too moist, and they run the risk of mould and mildew threatening the health of the staff.

The last time the maintenance crew reset the air system, the morons set the humidity level too low; Jake had a bloody nose and headache for three days.

Jake heard the rustling again, and then gurgling.

Gurgling? That gurgling was here in the hallway, not in the air vents.

Jake felt a drop of sweat release from the pit of his arm and run down his right side.

I have a Master's Degree in Astrophysics from the University of Western Ontario; I am an elite technician working in a billion dollar state of the art neutrino laboratory. I am NOT afraid of the dark.

Jake exhaled, his breath fluttering out. He took another small step. The gurgle got louder. It sounded closer.

Jake thought about sprinting to the control room, locking the door and grabbing his flash light. But he wasn't sure if he left the door half open, and being submerged in complete blackness, with his luck, he would run straight into the edge of the door.

You pussy, get a hold of yourself. You are in an old nickel mine two kilometers in the Earth's crust. It's probably minor seismic shifts that carry on all the time. With the lights out, heightened senses are just noticing them more.

"Ya, that makes sense," he said to himself.

Jake tried to swallow and reassure himself, but his mouth had dried. He moved his tongue along his teeth trying to produce a little saliva, but it wasn't working. More sweat started perspiring under his extended arm and he wiped off a few beads that began forming on his forehead.

He took another step. He rolled his foot (heel-to-toe), subconsciously trying to step as quietly as he could. There was more rustling and another gurgle less than one meter directly in front of him. Then Jake felt cold air engulf him, as if the blackened hallway had somehow transported him to an opened entrance of a walk-in freezer. But the cold wasn't refreshing. It didn't cause his pores to close in an automatic response to retain his body heat. On the contrary, he began to sweat even more. The muscles in his arms, fingers and legs started to involuntarily quiver. He could even feel the cold on the inside, and yet sweat was stinging his eyes.

His mind raced with no particular coherent thought. He felt he needed to run for his life. But to where? Logically, he knew the hallway extended a total of 30 metres in a straight, unhindered direction. He knew that he had approximately fifteen meters in front of him and fifteen meters behind him. The absolute darkness and his intense fear shifted his sense of direction. It altered how he viewed his physical space on the planet, as if he was floating in an infinite bubble with blackness in all directions. Alone.

Although his right hand was touching the counterfeit window, his brain was no longer connected to that reality.

Then, Jake heard it: a voice just inches in front of him. The voice was as sharp and as piercing as the cold phantom mist emanating from the same direction.

"So, Jakey," the *darkness* casually toyed, it's voice gritty. "You hate your life?"

Jake physically felt his heart skip a beat. The voice may have originated in front of him, but it seemed to have surrounded him. As if the darkness itself had come alive and was now talking, no — communicating — directly into his head.

I must be having some kind of psychotic breakdown, he tried to rationalize.

"I don't blame you," the *darkness* continued. "That whore got pregnant on purpose. She never would have graduated;

she is too much of a bimbo for that. And she was one party away from being flat broke. Then she saw you there, drunk and gullible. She may have been way out of your league, but she was desperate, Jakey, and you were horny."

The voice was so clear and focused. Being this far down inside the earth, entombed in this kind of darkness, seemed to suspend Jake's disbelief the same way a viewer would choose to when watching an unrealistic scene in a movie, allowing a disembodied voice seem somehow plausible.

And the voice was right. Jake thought he made the moves on her, using his witty one-liners to get between her legs. He even bragged about it to his friends. But now he was remembering it the right way — the way it had really happened.

He didn't "wham-bam-thank-you-ma'am" her and carried on his merry way. No. She had targeted him. She took *him* for the ride.

"She said she was on the pill, Jakey," the *darkness* taunted and twisted his memory. "She said she had never slept with a man she didn't know so quickly before."

Yes, I remember. She did say that.

"She talked you into cumming inside her. Not that it took much convincing; you're not all that bright, Jake. You didn't even grade top in your class. The Jet Propulsion Laboratories are for the elite in your field, not for idiots like you, Jake.

You are lucky, Jake Rogus, that you were able to con your way into working here. At least now you can send your paycheques back to that whore and her kid."

The words in Jake's head manipulated and guided his thoughts, funneling him deep into the darkness of personal loathing and defeat, converting the Creighton Mine into a two thousand metre crater of self-pity.

"Your life, Jake, I can give it back to you. I can make all this shit go away, just like it never happened," the *darkness* said, its tone softened, sounding more human.

Jake lowered his right arm; his fingers slid down the glass and over the frame of the window sill to eventually rest at his side.

"You can?" Jake asked aloud to the blackness. "How?"

"Oh Jakey, as a team we can do anything, everything. We'll start by telling the whore to fuck off. Then we'll tell that whore's brat to fuck off."

For the first time in almost a year, Jake's spirits began to rise.

"Ya," he replied aloud. Somehow he felt taller, stronger.

"Ya," he reconfirmed. He could feel his self confidence rise and as it did, the hate for his screwed up life also grew.

"Yes Jake, that's it," the *darkness* encouraged. "And the first thing we'll do is tell this hole in the ground to fuck off. We'll march right into that director's office — hopefully he's in a meeting — and we'll beat the shit out of him. Real scientists don't work like this, scurrying around like moles in tunnels under ground. "

"No, we don't," Jake yelled. Fire burned in his chest. His legs tensed, ready to spring forward and sprint to the elevator.

"We're going to be sitting on a beach, Jakey, in Southern California, soaking up the sun, getting a tan, drinking pina-coladas, looking at perky tits walking by, and solving the Universe's equations that the JPL boys just can't wrap their little brains around."

"Ya, that's what I wanna do," Jake agreed.

"And we're gonna Jakey, right now. Right this instant."

A small insignificant voice in the back of Jake Rogus's subconscious chirped one word that fluttered the energy in his legs; that threatened the burning in his chest. It was a realization that was about to tumble his dreams like a house built by a deck of cards: *How?*

"Just open your mouth," the *darkness* instructed.

My mouth?

"Stop fighting it Jake. Let's show the world what Jake Rogus can be, who Jake Rogus really is. To hell with that bitch and her kid. To hell with this shitty job. To hell Jake."

Yeah.

He felt his legs pulsate with adrenaline. The hate flared up in his chest. He felt good, strong.

"To hell with them all," he said back to the *darkness*.

Then, Jake Rogus opened his mouth.

CHAPTER TWENTY

Dartmouth General Hospital,
Dartmouth Nova Scotia

Janice Baudelaire has been working at the Dartmouth General as a Registered Nurse for eighteen years, and even though she is overworked and stressed out, she still manages to show up at work with a smile on her face, usually wearing scrubs decorated in one of the season's festive characters. At Christmas, Janice dressed up as Mrs. Claus (red scrubs, Santa hat). At Easter, she wore bunny ears with a scrubs printed full of colourful Easter eggs. Today, with June 21 rapidly approaching, Janice's scrubs display miniature Stonehenges and an overall druid motif. As Janice whisked past Curtis's door, she looked in and noticed that he was sitting on the edge of his bed.

"What do you think you're doing?" she scorned him. "You have to lie back down. As soon as Dr. Greggory has a minute, he'll come in and talk to you."

"No, I'm good," Curtis argued. "Just-take out this I.V. here... the needle is *really* scratching up the inside of my arm."

"That's because you are supposed to be lying down," the

nurse fired back while she put pressure on his shoulder trying to persuade him to lay back into bed.

"I appreciate the care you have given me and my daughter, but I need to go, now," he said trying desperately to keep the panic out of his voice.

Holding out his arm, he looked down at the I.V. sticking out of his arm and then back at the nurse.

"Would you...?" he motioned to the needle.

"No! Mr. Papp, you have just been hit by a car. You have two broken and two cracked ribs, and both of your feet are bruised and swollen. You may think you feel okay right now, but that is because we have you pumped with 2 mg of Dilaudid. And we're still waiting on x-Ray results to see if there is any internal damage."

Curtis stayed sitting up and stared into the face of the frustrated nurse.

"Honey," the nurse said bending down to Charlie, "can you please tell your daddy to grow up and be a big boy and stay in the hospital so we can take care of him."

Charlie raised her palms up and shrugged her shoulders. "He can be pretty stubborn at times."

Curtis shook his head at his daughter and reached over with his I.V.'d arm and messed Charlie's hair.

Ouch... He bit his lip as pain shot up his arm, across his shoulder and through his chest, immediately he regretted doing it. The pain was almost enough to change his mind and lay back down in the bed.

Eavery stood up and walked over to the foot of the bed. "Don't you worry, Miss; we'll take care of him."

The nurse exhaled in frustration.

"I will give the doctor a call and have him come right over. It will take him about an hour if you're lucky. In the meantime, just sit back and relax. And you'll have to fill out an AMA (Against Medical Advice) form, absolving the hospital and staff of any injuries that you will probably incur by prematurely leaving the Intensive Care Unit."

"An hour?" Eavery asked disgustedly. "Why would it take an hour to have the doctor walk over? Is he in surgery?"

"An hour?" Curtis echoed. "Couldn't you send another doctor over?"

"No," she said, frustration clearly visible on her face. She may have been a smiling, happy nurse at the beginning of her shift, but that nurse was gone now.

"We have one doctor for the entire ICU, plus he has to do his rounds on another floor. Welcome to Canada's Health Care system."

Curtis scratched his arm where the inner catheter probed under his skin.

"Fine," she said, grabbing Curtis's arm she pulled out the intravenous tubing, catheter and support tape in one fluid motion. Curtis couldn't tell what hurt more: the needle being torn from his arm, the tape being torn off his skin (taking some hair with it), or the sudden jerk the nurse gave him.

"They brought you and your daughter in by ambulance; you have no idea how lucky she was not getting hurt," the nurse said, using guilt as her last chance to keep Curtis in the hospital.

I have some idea, he thought.

Nurse Baudelaire poured Curtis a glass of water from the pitcher. "I want you to drink some water before you go home which, I am telling you, is a very bad idea. I will go and get your papers to sign."

As the nurse left his room, Sergeant O'Connell walked in.

Oh great!

"Sarge, what are you doing here?" Curtis said sitting up taller, thankful the Dilaudid had kicked in.

"My office got a call from the hospital saying you were

admitted. It is standard procedure once they have I.D.'d you as military." He looked Curtis over.

"How are you doing? They mentioned you were in that accident downtown."

"Good," Curtis lied. "Just really stiff. That van just missed us."

"Thank God," the sergeant said and exhaled. He bent down on one knee. "And what about you Charlie, are you okay too?"

"Yeah, I'm okay," Charlie whispered shyly, not too sure who the man in the camouflage green uniform was.

"Good," Sergeant O'Connell said authentically relieved. Standing back up he looked around, "Where's Vivica?"

"She's gone to Ireland. A university field trip."

"Who is going to look after you and Charlie at home?"

Curtis motioned toward Eavery. "I got a buddy here who will check up on me."

Sergeant O'Connell suspiciously looked over in Eavery's direction.

"I want you to go to the Infirmary on base tomorrow and have our doctors look at you. I will give you as much time off as you need to recover — don't worry yourself about that. Have you got a ride home?"

"I left my car back at Alderney Landing, but Eavery here will drive me down." Curtis felt bad for lying to his sergeant, but he definitely didn't feel like explaining anything right now — or ever.

"Alright," the sergeant said. "But I will need a 663 report of the incident done up as soon as you can. Plus the M.P.s are going to want a statement about what happened — they can share it with the Halifax Regional Police."

"No problem," Curtis quickly replied doing his best to sound strong, although his head was spinning and vomit was working its way to the surface.

After an hour of getting dressed and signing the AMA

form, Curtis, Charlie and Eavery waited downstairs for the taxi. Eavery watched as it turned off Pleasant Street and headed towards the hospital. He looked over at Curtis who was leaning against the stone embedded pillar.

"So after we pick up your car, what's the first thing you want to do?" Eavery asked.

Curtis's stomach was nauseated from the medication. "Get a Timmy's."

"A Timmy's? You want a coffee now?" Eavery questioned.

"Yeah, I haven't had one all day. My head is pounding," Curtis replied.

Eavery laughed and shook his head in disbelief. "You Military are all the same: gotta have your Timmy's."

"Well, of course we do," Curtis said in a flat and candid tone. "Why do you think we have one in Afghanistan? Rumour has it," he continued, "that the Minister of Defense is pushing the Vatican to canonize Tim Horton as the Patron Saint of Coffee."

Curtis laughed out loud at his own joke. "Ohhh, I shouldn't have laughed," Curtis said and he grabbed his head and closed his eyes.

"You know, I wouldn't doubt it," Eavery chuckled.

"Daddy, here's our taxi," Charlie interrupted as the car pulled up.

Charlie helped Curtis into the cab. "On second thought, let's just go straight home. We can get the car tomorrow. "

"Do you know of any good Nephilim that do rapid healing?" Curtis quietly half joked as the cab pulled out of the hospital onto Pleasant Street and headed towards Eastern Passage.

"None that I can think of," Eavery said.

"What about saints? There has got to be a patron saint I can flash a prayer to for quick recovery or something like that?" Curtis asked, feeling the throbbing in his feet and chest return.

"Ah, ya, Saint Rita or Saint Joseph, but I am not really a saint person," Eavery opened up.

"No, really, why is that?"

"Because there is a bloody patron saint for everything, I find it ridiculous. Florists have St. Dorothy, gunners in the army have St. Barbara — you know I don't have a problem with the military," Eavery looked over at Curtis, "but really, a patron saint so a gunner can more effectively kill someone?"

Curtis didn't take any offence to Eavery's opinion, but he thought if he was stuck in a battle, he wouldn't mind praying to someone to help get his ass back home.

"Well, they are the enemy," Curtis tossed in.

"Enemies change as fast as governments," Eavery lectured.

Curtis had no intention of getting into that conversation, although he did agree with Eavery on that point.

"Even the most hated man in the Old and New Testament — the tax man — has a Vatican approved patron saint; St. Matthew," Eavery continued. "Saints — at best — are just good people who the Vatican uses as pawns to help gain support in a specific region…"

"I wish I never asked," Curtis said looking down at Charlie.

"And," Eavery continued, "praying is more than just chanting some words or blankly reading a script typed out by the rectory. Actual praying is a focus of using the divine spark and essentially creating *D-E*."

"D-E?" Curtis asked blankly, his head no longer into the discussion.

"d,e,f,g,h,i…" Charlie sang breaking into the Alphabet song, reminding everyone she was still in the car.

"Sorry, Divine Energy. Then you channel that energy to a specific angel, god or divine being. That energy strengthens them, and in return they might do what you've asked."

Curtis did a quick inward reflection. Wow — how his life has changed! All of the things he has seen, heard and learned in the last few days have altered him enough so he can now have a full blown discussion of *D-E*, gods, angels, and god-knows-what else in the back of cab as openly and uninhibitedly as talking about politics and gasoline prices.

In the distance he could hear Eavery continue.

"Many gods and divine beings get addicted to that energy and that's why you find many of the same gods jumping pantheons. Sometimes they change their outward appearance and take on new roles and other times they just take on a new name. It all depends on the tribe or civilization that has become connected to them. Ares, for instance, was the Greek god of war, and he is also Mars, the Roman god of war. He later became Gabriel, the Archangel of vengeance and death."

"What?" Curtis chuckled, feeling light headed and giddy from the Dilaudid.

"Well," Eavery stammered, "he also has other responsibilities. He's the angel of resurrection and mercy. And he set the Prophet Mohammad on his path, creating Islam. Egyptian deities, too, bounced all over the place. Osiris was initially the God of Nature. Then, he became the God of the Dead. As the Egyptian pantheons died out, he took over as Hades, then Pluto. The Egyptians worshipped the Earth God, Geb; the Druids had Gaia. The Celtic god Dagda was the King of all Gods, as was Zeus and Odin. The Egyptian Eset was the Mother of God as is Mary in the Christian pantheon. And the Egyptian god Thoth, the God of Wisdom and Knowledge, is no other than your divine ancestor Jophiel."

Eavery paused letting this new insight sink in. By the look on Curtis's face he was struggling to keep up.

"I'm not trying to shoot a dead horse here," Eavery said taking a breather. "Pop culture has done god comparisons to death it is hardly some new revelation. My point is, the divine are dynamic; they bounce around, addicted to prayers and the divine energy that humans give them. So use your prayers wisely."

Curtis noticed the cabbie had been watching them from the rear view mirror and consistently pushed himself back into his seat, listening to their conversation. Then suspicion flirted with Curtis's intuition. With the very recent murder of Brent and his family, and the obvious intelligence network of the KRÁJCÁR within the Halifax area, a cabbie would make an excellent field agent.

Curtis did not want this possible snitch knowing his home address.

"On second thought," Curtis said leaning towards the driver, "drop us off at the Value Grocer; there are some things I need to get."

"No problem," the cabbie acknowledged.

"Are you serious?" Eavery questioned. "You can't walk home from there."

Curtis leaned in close to Eavery's ear and filled him in on his suspicions. Skepticism panned across Eavery's face, but with all that has happened recently, maybe a little more vigilance is a good idea.

The walk home from the village grocery store was slow and arduous; Curtis limped the entire way using Charlie as a human crutch.

"You can put more weight on me daddy; I can take it," she squeezed out between a scrunched face and squinting eyes.

"I am, Peanut," Curtis replied. Of course he wasn't and the throbbing pain throughout his feet and shins reflected it. Eavery opened the door ahead of Curtis and helped him up the three concrete steps into the house and onto the chesterfield.

As soon as he sat down and put his feet up on the pillows, Curtis could feel his bones settle and sink into the soft folds and fabric of the cushions. Contented, his body relaxed.

Eavery took a self-guided tour of the Papp home.

"Do you want some water or something?" he called from the kitchen.

"Nope. Doing good."

All he needed was to relax and let the tides of exhaustion wash away the day's events.

Returning to the living room, satisfied with his recce, Eavery settled himself into a large reclining chair just opposite the couch.

Eavery watched Charlie pull three *My Little Pony* dolls out of her toy box near the window.

"We're going to have a dance party today, Star Catcher," Charlie said to her plastic figurine.

"Do you like ponies Charlie?" Eavery asked the young Papp.

"Oh, very much," Charlie answered, not taking her eyes off her toys. "Ponies and horses are my favourite."

"Horses?" Eavery persisted. "You like horses, do you?"

"Oh, very much," Charlie echoed as she continued to have a pony dance party.

Eavery looked around the room for something entertaining and found an old T.V. set propped up on a refurbished bookcase filled with a VHS recorder and dozens of children's VHS tapes in the corner.

"Is that your T.V.?" Eavery asked Curtis, almost insulted by the lack of modern technology within the household.

Curtis opened his eyes to slits and looked over at his television.

"Of course it is," Curtis returned hearing the tone of disapproval in Eavery's voice. "What's wrong with it?"

Eavery looked over into the other corner of the room where a beat-up desktop computer with a 13 inch CRT monitor rested on a rolling computer desk.

Eavery leaned forward and, resting his elbows on his knees, looked into Curtis's slit eyes.

"Let me see if I understand you. You are a communications technician for the military. You work on and with satellite phones and data systems linking the world's superpowers with Ottawa. You manage and repair computers and all their software on a daily basis and you don't even own a cell phone of any kind? Your television was built in the eighties and your home computer probably couldn't handle high-speed internet. What am I missing here? Are you a technophobe?"

Curtis opened his eyes again and repositioned a throw pillow under his head so he didn't have to strain himself to look at Eavery.

"Just because I am not a slave to technology does not mean I have technophobia. I am surrounded by it daily. I don't have a cell phone, BlackBerry or iPhone because I don't want one. It is actually liberating being 'unplugged' from everyone and everything when I am just going for a walk or driving down the road. I don't appreciate getting calls and texts throughout my day. I have witnessed time and time again, people who have cell phones can't turn them off — not even to drive their vehicles. There are more accidents caused by drivers paying too much attention to their phones while in traffic than alcohol and drugs combined in Canada. It has become a true addiction.

As for my T.V., sure it's not new, but it works fine. And it may not have a 1,000,000:1 contrast ratio, but it was free and I can watch all my documentaries, Vivica can watch her *CSI: New York* and Charlie can watch her videos."

Eavery sat back in his chair, not prepared for the chastising lecture and realized he had just poked an issue Curtis probably defends often.

"Point is," Curtis continued, "sure it's old, but today you can't buy anything *new*; the moment you've walked out of the store with your T.V. still in the box, its already five minutes old and some else is walking out behind you with a newer, better model. It is a cycle of consumerism we don't contribute to."

"You're not going tree hugger on me, are you Curtis?" Eavery jabbed.

"No!" Curtis chuckled. "I just don't like wasting my money."

Curtis pulled the pillow out and laid his head back down. "You are right about one thing, Eavery."

"What's that?" Eavery asked, feeling a little sheepish like a child that had been scorned.

"My computer, it can't take high speed internet," Curtis laughed aloud again and once again immediately regretted it.

Eavery also laughed aloud, sensing Curtis's hurt feelings were on the mend, and glad that his boorish assault didn't wound Curtis too deeply.

Charlie walked over and placed her ponies on the coffee table across from Curtis.

"You need your sleep daddy," Charlie whispered as she knelt beside him and played with her father's hair. Curtis could feel his mind being tugged and pulled out of his body with each gentle caress of the child's little fingers. As he started to drift off, his thoughts were escorted by the sound of the four year old voice singing a lullaby. Curtis couldn't quite make out which lullaby Charlie was singing; it sounded as if she was singing three or four at the same time. The circling of her fingers on his forehead and the soft chanting transformed the sofa Curtis was resting on into a Venusians' Gondola drifting lazily down a glutinous river of milk and honey, gently yawing and rolling. The pain in Curtis's chest, feet and head melted off of him like the condensation running down the outside of a glass of ice water. The further the Gondola carried Curtis down the river, the less he heard his daughter's voice and the less the Gondola yawed and rolled. Time and space seemed to have collapsed in on itself, and Curtis noticed; so did the pain. Within the absolute sense of tranquility and comfort that Curtis had never before experienced, or knew was even possible, he could no longer judge if he was still lying down or standing.

He envisioned himself in a kind of suspended animation, like being completely submerged in a warm bath. The slight activity still registering through Curtis's brain tugged at his first-developed memories of a forming fetus securely engulfed in his mother's womb.

As quickly as his revelation bloomed, it withered. A violent and disturbing sensation was rapidly overtaking his euphoria. A rhythmic and abrasive sound penetrated the membrane that had cocooned him in his trance. He once again became aware of the physical boundaries of the Gondola as it began to pitch and rock — not forcefully, but definitely without welcome.

The coarse throttling sound, resembling the garroted honking of wild geese, flooded Curtis's ears and head, rapidly drawing him to the surface of the dream world. As the realization of the sofa's physical dimensions, with its sags and lumps of the sofa anchored themselves, Curtis awoke with a startled confusion.

Charlie and Eavery were standing at the foot of the couch laughing. Curtis's heart pounded heavily in his chest and a dense fog suspended itself in his mind. Curtis sat there looking at these two strangers laughing at him. The chorus of wild honks faded as the fog burned off.

"Daddy," Charlie laughed, clearly entertained. "You were snoring — loudly."

"What? Who?" Curtis looked around.

Couch. Living room. He could barely remember coming home.

Suddenly, the world around him came into focus. Curtis shifted and finally sat up.

"Man, you were out cold," Eavery said through a smile.

Sphinx gave a timid meow and leapt onto Curtis's lap.

"Yeah, thanks to Charlie," Curtis said giving her a wink and stroked the cat.

Eavery took a step closer and nonchalantly looked Curtis over.

"You look better. You even have some colour in your cheeks. How are you feeling?"

Curtis took a deep breath, inflated his lungs and expanded his chest. A majority of his pain was gone. His chest was tight and if he tried hard enough he could probably bring some of the pain back to the surface, but with all consideration, he felt a lot better — even good, perhaps.

Wiggling his toes, he tapped the floor with the pads of his feet. Nothing; no pain.

"Amazing! Those drugs really work. It's about time they kicked in," Curtis said as relief spread across his face.

"I might be going back to work tomorrow."

"I don't know about that," Eavery said as he slid down on the couch next to Curtis.

Charlie walked up with a smile on her face and grabbed Sphinx off of Curtis's lap. In a classic rag doll form, Sphinx let his body go limp as Charlie tucked both forearms around his chest and bear walked the cat to a pile of doll clothes, his tail dragging on the floor between her steps.

"I'm glad you are feeling better daddy, now me and Mrs. Flowerpeddles are going to get dressed for a tea party."

Both Curtis and Eavery chuckled at the shame Sphinx was surely about to endure.

"Well," Curtis said looking over at Eavery, "when he's had enough he usually bolts for safety under our bed."

"And there is no leaving early today, Mrs. Flowerpeddles. I closed mommy's door," Charlie told Sphinx as she pushed one of her doll's pink tutus over his head.

"Oh, that cat is going to need a stiff drink," Eavery

remarked as he watched the unnatural transformation of a house cat to a ballerina.

Turning his attention back to Curtis, Eavery examined him sideways, not sure how to judge his recovery or if he should express his thoughts. Speaking slowly, he carefully chose his words.

"I think your recovery — you feeling better and in less pain — was more likely caused by actual healing than the pills the hospital gave you."

"What? Are you telling me that when I fell asleep you broke down and asked a favour from Gabriel or someone?"

"No," Eavery said, pausing.

"So you think healing may be one of my gifts that I am learning to use?" Curtis said, feeling his ego inflate at the thought of healing as a superpower.

"No," Eavery repeated. "When you were sleeping, I watched Charlie as she played with your hair. Her aura flared as she started to chant. That's when you passed out."

"Wait a second," Curtis said, trying to collect himself. "Did you just say Charlie has an aura? And it what? It flared?"

Eavery repositioned on the sofa. "Yeah, I saw it the moment I met her. You mean *you* have never seen it?"

Curtis looked over to the door where Charlie had walked out of the room holding Sphinx. His head felt heavy, like it was full of sand.

"No, I never have," he said, mostly to himself. "And it flared?" he questioned, returning his attention back to Eavery.

"When she started to chant," Eavery reclaimed. "At first it sounded like she was singing, "Row, Row, Row Your Boat," but then it morphed into a *melodic* choir. It was quite beautiful."

"I heard it," Curtis replied. "It carried me off into the most peaceful sleep of my life."

"That's when her aura flared. Earlier it was a simple peach colour, and then it flared and engulfed the two of you."

Curtis stood up and wiggled his toes. He then ran his fingers across his ribs.

"And now all of my pain is gone. I bet you that an x-ray would prove my ribs have healed." Curtis turned and looked down at Eavery still sitting on the sofa.

"Have you ever heard of healing like that? Just — *bam* — you wake up and your broken bones are healed?"

"Of course," Eavery answered plainly. "There are literally thousands of people in the world today that can heal with their hands, or by chanting, or with some kind of intense focus. A majority of them become doctors and specialists. They probably don't even realize they have these gifts; to them they just have patients with abnormally high recovering rates."

As if on cue, Charlie walked in holding Mrs. Flowerpeddles, the Ballerina. While the cat hung suspended in her arms like a cooked noodle, Charlie smiled and looked up at her daddy. Curtis stared down at his daughter, still unable to see her aura and feeling the cold trickle of insecurity and wounded pride of being left out of a family secret. Somewhere in the distance, Curtis could hear the voice of his little daughter relentlessly questioning the status of his health.

"Curtis?" Eavery said interrupting his thoughts. "Are you okay?"

"Yes? Yes!" Curtis said looking over at Eavery and then at Charlie. As if being splashed with cold water, Curtis snapped out of his self-pity and came back to reality. Slowly bending down on one knee, he gave Charlie and Mrs. Flowerpeddles a hug.

"I am feeling waaaay better. Thank you very, very much. You will have to show me how you did that someday."

"Okay, daddy," Charlie said through a large smile. "Come on Mrs. Flowerpeddles, it's time for our tea party."

Sensing his own misfortune, Sphinx bellowed an unenthused meow and allowed himself to be carried off to tea.

"So when Charlie was born, was she a bit different?" Eavery asked, watching Curtis trudge gingerly to the kitchen.

"Different? How do you mean?" Curtis questioned as he pulled this morning's pot from the coffee maker and give it a swirl. He offered some to Eavery. Eavery looked at the black soup and declined. *Oh well*, Curtis thought and poured himself a cup. Then he leaned back and rested against the kitchen counter, holding his cup in both hands.

"Was she born with unusual features? Like 11 or 12 fingers or all of her teeth?"

Eavery watched Curtis's expression change from questioning to shock.

"Yeah, she *was* born with all her teeth. It was really weird, I mean, she was a beautiful baby, and she still is, but a newborn screaming in the delivery room with a mouth full of teeth! The doctor called them 'natal teeth.' He said it was very rare — 1 in 3000 births. He had never seen it before, only read about it. Vivica said it made breast feeding interesting."

Curtis's eyes refocused from the feeding memories (which *he* found slightly comical, but then again it wasn't his nipples being chewed on) back to Eavery.

"Why did you ask that? How did you know?"

Eavery leaned his right shoulder against the fridge. "Charlie is a Táltos."

"A *Táltos*?" Curtis searched his mind for the word. "A Táltos? I've never heard of it."

"The Táltos are Hungarian healers. As children they are born with an oddity; like extra fingers or a mouth full of teeth. In the womb, they are said to be directly linked to God and when they are born they are fully aware of the world around them. They also mature faster because of it."

Curtis took another sip of his cold, brutally strong coffee, remembering his "old soul" theory relating to Charlie.

"So they're healers?" Curtis half asked and half stated.

"That would explain your miraculous recovery," Eavery said, waving his hand from Curtis's head to his toes.

"So the Táltos can heal people, and even mend broken bones," Curtis said mostly to himself. He was trying desperately to grasp his daughter's complexity.

"Is she a Táltos because I am a Nephilim?"

"No, I don't think so. I have never known one whose parents were half angel."

"You've known other Táltos?" Curtis asked, feeling his daughter's uniqueness waiver.

"Oh, all kinds, but I haven't seen any for a really long time."

"Are the KRÁJCÁR hunting them down too?" Curtis asked, his jaw tight with anger.

"No, actually it was Christianity."

"Pardon?"

"King Stephen I of Hungary, back in 1000 A.D., began converting the Magyar tribes from their pagan beliefs to Christianity. He persecuted the Táltos as witches and started the world's first witch hunt, wiping out thousands of these divine healers, many right at birth. Since then the Táltos — the true Táltos — are non-existent... practically." Eavery shook his head. "But he got his sainthood out of it. Szent Istvan," he exhaled.

Coming back to the present, Curtis noticed he was turning his cup in circles.

"So the Táltos — they chant and talk to God, and heal people?" Curtis asked, thinking back to Charlie's intervention with him on the couch.

"Yep! They are on a level most humans couldn't understand.

She could make a strong, powerful ally in a world against the KRÁJCÁR."

The very thought of exploiting his Charlie offended Curtis.

"She is my four year old daughter; I will give my life to protect her," Curtis blurted, surprised at Eavery's callous statement.

"Of course, Curtis," Eavery pulled back. "But she is growing up in a world within a world. And your world — her world — has real angels, real demons, and real assassins. She may be a four year old on the outside, playing tea party with her dolls and learning how to use the potty, but on the inside she is a *divine* superpower."

"What am I going to do? What are we going to do?" Curtis asked, feeling the true weight of his situation pull on him. The idea of someone going out of their way to hurt or kill Charlie filled his mind with unwanted and indescribable images. Deep inside, his self-control was slipping to the point of panic. Not to mention the fact that the world has changed and Vivica was still unaware of any of it.

"Right now they don't know you," Eavery said, trying to sow some calm into Curtis.

"But they will!" Curtis blurted, his chest tight. "You know, in the military we are trained to face and fight the enemy. But when the enemy can be anyone — your grocer, your cab driver, your friggin' neighbour — and they're targeting your family, how can you fight that? Where do you make your stand?"

"Well, the first thing, Curtis, is training," Eavery said, trying to put Curtis at ease. "Remember that feeling you got before the van hit you? How you practically froze time and moved out of the way? That is only part of your abilities."

That makes sense, Curtis thought to himself. He put the cup of cold coffee down and stood up straight, still amazed how good he felt.

Yeah, training!

"If they don't know me yet, at least I have that up on them. So training, how do we do that?"

Eavery wasn't sure; in fact, he was stalled on that issue. He lowered his eyes, "I don't know."

Curtis stared blankly at Eavery. He could feel the bubbling of panic again.

"Wow, you're a lot of help. How have you managed? What have you been doing all these years?"

"Me?" Eavery paused with some self-reflection. "I move around a lot, but I'm not really on the KRÁJCÁR radar."

Curtis watched Eavery become uncomfortable, his posture sinking, as if he was trying to hide himself in plain sight.

"You're not? Why? How have you managed that?" Curtis felt some hope fill in a little of the hole that the stress was creating.

Again, Curtis watched Eavery awkwardly search for his words.

"They are not as interested in my heritage as much as yours. But, perhaps you could talk to Jophiel; maybe there is something he can do?"

Curtis watched Eavery with suspicion for a few seconds and then guilt mixed itself in with the tumultuous cocktail of emotions.

The stress is causing me to question the very nature of my friend, he thought to himself.

"Jophiel!" Curtis said aloud triumphantly, as if solving some great equation. "Do you think he would help?"

"I don't know!"

Curtis felt the rapidly eroding foundation beneath his feet solidify just a little.

"Have the Cherubim helped a lot of people in the past?" he asked, hoping for some positive news.

"Not that I am aware of," Eavery garbled, running his fingers over his mouth at the same time.

A little more foundation eroded.

Curtis felt the tingle of electricity in the air. Then the hair on the back of his neck straightened, reminding him that he needed a hair cut before he went back to work. Then he watched the hair on his arms rise. A curious look popped onto Eavery's face and both of them looked around the kitchen. A second later, the now familiar sound of discharging electricity filled the house. Fingers of platinum-coloured plasma arced along the floor, across the cupboards and counter top, up the stove and along the door of the fridge. Pictures and drawings Charlie coloured at daycare fell to the floor as the current neutralized the cheap magnets that held them to the appliances. Finally, there was a thunderous *crack*, a flash of white light, and the distinct smell of ozone.

Curtis and Eavery stood motionless, waiting for someone to appear. Then the black Cherubim with the silver ribbons swirling beneath his skin entered the kitchen from the living room, behind Eavery. Still standing modestly tall with his wings folded behind his back, Jophiel approached them. Where the satchel and scroll once sat on his left hip there was now a gleaming golden scabbard and sword. As he entered the kitchen, he had to duck his head and twist his back to fit himself through the doorframe. Eavery stepped to the side to give the angelic being more room.

Standing in front of the two men, Jophiel looked down directly at Curtis, stared into him, read him, every fiber, and every thought.

The silver ribbons under the Cherubim's skin began to mix and swirl faster, more energized, almost chaotic.

Jophiel placed his left hand on top of the handle of his sword, glanced over at Eavery and then slowly back at Curtis.

"I'll do it."

About the Author

Kirk Allen Kreitzer is a corporal in the Canadian Air force presently stationed in Halifax, NS, at 12 Wing Shearwater. Kirk has a loving (and patient) wife, Lisa and a very comical and rambunctious five year old daughter, Alexsys. I decided to venture into the world of writing because my wife and I were bored with the books that were out there. I have been looking for a supernatural thriller that is uniquely Canadian, and when I couldn't find one (perhaps I was looking in the wrong places), I decided to write one. After many proof reads by friends and family, they urged me to bring Curits Papp alive for the public to read. I hope you enjoy it.

CPSIA information can be obtained
at www.ICGtesting.com
Printed in the USA
LVHW091120250222
712011LV00003B/60